A Yeti for the Holidays

Jade Dara

To our group chat, *A Court of Memes and Manhoods*

Author's Note

It has taken me over four years to write and finalize this little book, often working through a lot of self-doubt and anxiety due to perfectionism. In the end, I realized that I'm standing in my own way, and it doesn't have to be perfect to be fun and enjoyable. It definitely is not perfect, and I love it anyways.

It is my hope that this book is read in the spirit of what it is intended to be: a fluffy monster romance novel with a giant cinnamon roll of a yeti that doesn't take itself too seriously.

Triggers may include: mention of death of a parent, loneliness, light stalking, explicit scenes, monster peen, slight possessiveness/jealousy of MMC.

This is not a cute, cuddly book for children.

Grammar triggers may include: excessive use of hyphens. I love a hyphen, and I'm not ashamed to say it.

Chapter 1

Stefania

"I'm sorry, what did you say?"

Stefania shifted the grocery bags full of half-price Halloween candy to one hand and cradled the phone against her cheek with the other. She closed the front door of her Seattle condo with a booted foot as the bored voice on the other line intoned, "Your great-uncle passed away and left you his property here in Alaska. We'll need for you to come up to Winterhaven and sign the paperwork as soon as possible."

Stefania maneuvered through her tiny foyer to the kitchen and set the grocery bags on the counter with a *thump*. So she *had* heard correctly the first time. "This has to be a mistake, as I don't have a great-uncle. I don't have any family left at all."

The voice on the other end of the line sighed. What was their name? Jocelyn? Jasmine? Jeanine? Stefania hadn't paid enough attention when she'd answered the phone, and it served her right for accidentally accepting a call from an unknown Alaskan number. Why were the accept/decline options so close together on phone screens? Maybe she'd write a strongly worded letter

1

to the manufacturer to insist they change the interface.

"You confirmed that you are indeed Stefania Anne Clarke, daughter of Lily Anne Clarke, correct?"

Stefania closed her eyes and placed a hand on her chest, forcing herself to take two deep inhales before she replied. Seven years had gone by since her mother's death, the pain of her sudden absence barely fading with time. Hearing her mother's name never failed to make her heart feel as if it were cracking in two. Lily Clarke had been her best friend, her confidante, her everything. "Yes, that's me. But she never mentioned having an uncle. She would've told me."

"Well, she did have an uncle, Miss Clarke, whether she knew it or not. Her father had a brother, Charles Clarke, who passed away two weeks ago." Stefania figured the voice on the phone must call surviving relatives often as they spoke with such clinical disinterest. "And according to the letter Charles left with our firm, you are his sole remaining heir. I'm sorry to have to tell you this over the phone, but we're trying to settle his estate as soon as possible."

Stefania felt as if her brain was encapsulated in fog. It was Friday and her mind was already mush from a long work-week, and now to add this on top of it? A great-uncle. All those years of thinking she didn't have a family and as it turns out, she had a great-uncle. *Well, not anymore,* she supposed, her dark humor briefly flashing to the surface. "Why didn't he ever try to contact me? How do you even have my number?"

The voice let out another long-suffering sigh, clearly wanting the conversation to end. Stefania figured she must be the last call of the day. "Miss Clarke, that information was not divulged to us. I'm sorry to tell you about your great-uncle's death, but can I make an appointment for you for next week? I'm not authorized to give you any more information over the phone."

Stefania made an appointment for the following Tuesday afternoon in a daze and ended the call. She went through the motions of putting away her groceries as her mind raced with the metaphorical bomb that had just been dropped on her. The half-priced chocolate (paired with a glass of red wine, of course) would come in handy tonight as she tried to process this news.

A great-uncle. Charles Clarke, *her great-uncle.*

Her mother Lily had never spoken of him- had she even known he existed? Nothing had been off limits between mother and daughter, as there was no subject not allowed, no topic too taboo. Lily would have told her if they had family. What had happened between Charles and the family to cause them to never speak of him? Was he a terrible man? An axe murderer? A conspiracy theorist? A recluse?

More importantly, he'd clearly known about her if he'd left these instructions with the law firm.

So why had he never contacted her?

She sighed as she cracked open her container of grocery-store sushi (she knew it was borderline sacrilege but she didn't feel like cooking) and opened the map app on her phone.

Where was Winterhaven, after all?

Several hours later, Stefania completed the submission for bereavement time-off from the Seattle-based technology company where she worked as a graphic designer and sat back against the couch.

She had spent most of the evening combing through social media sites and search engines but it had proved fruitless. She assumed the old man must've lived as off-the-grid as a person possibly could, as it was almost impossible in this day and age to *not* have a digital footprint. But nothing, not even an obituary, came up for a Charles Clarke living in Winterhaven, Alaska.

What had he been like? What did he look like? Did he have the signature red hair of the rest of the Clarke line? The same pale, freckled skin and tall, broad build? The legendary stubborn streak?

Stefania stood and stretched her arms overhead, feeling stiff after spending the evening hunched over her laptop. She had turned thirty-seven this year and sometimes felt every year in her bones- the hike she had planned for tomorrow would require some extra stretching before *and* afterwards. Padding down the hallway to her bedroom, she glanced at herself in the hallway mirror, pausing as she ran her hands down her sides and admired the cut of the belted sweater-dress she had worn for her client meeting today.

She herself had a lot of the typical Clarke genes: tall, pale, strongly-built, red hair. While her mother had been willowy, Stefania was voluptuous, with generous curves that had filled out seemingly overnight during high school and had never left. She turned and examined her profile in the mirror, admiring how amazing her ass looked in the dress. Maybe the curves came from the women on her father's side of the family- she'd probably never know.

Her mother Lily had gotten pregnant during her last semester of college, a brief fling with an exchange student from Sweden that had resulted in Stefania. By the time Lily had realized she was pregnant, Stefania's father had returned to Sweden leaving behind no last name and no method to contact him. Lily, brave and determined, raised Stefania on her own. Stefania had never even seen a photograph of her father, and her mother had rarely described him as anything other than tall, handsome, and charismatic. He was an enigma, one Stefania made peace with years ago with the help of therapy.

She had once entertained the idea of passing the family traits on to her own children one day, but she was still undecided as to whether she wanted them or not. Her years-long engagement to Doug (Doug the Drag as her friends had dubbed him in honor of his perpetually dour mood) had fallen through last year, shattering any thoughts she had about beginning a family with him. She had picked up the pieces of her life and transferred to Seattle where she briefly tried dating apps, but diving into that cesspool had been enough of a turnoff for her

4

that she'd sworn off trying to date seriously for at least another year or two.

So, no- children would most likely not be in her future, and that was fine. She could hear her coworker Shawna's voice in her mind: *Children? In this economy? No thanks!*

Tonight, she had learned that the small town of Winterhaven was nestled at the base of Denali (or Mt. McKinley as it was also known) and that the drive from Seattle was about forty-two hours. As pretty as that route would be through the Canadian Rockies, she instead booked a flight to the closest airport in Anchorage. From there, she would take a two-and-a-half-hour train ride into Winterhaven and hope that her great-uncle left a car she could use while she was there.

Stefania had no idea what the property was like or what shape the house was in, so she sent a mental request to the universe in hopes of at least finding a house with solid walls, a roof, and indoor plumbing. Did it even have internet and wi-fi? She made another note to look for a hotel in the area just in case the house was uninhabitable. If it was in terrible condition, she supposed she could try to clean it up as best she could and sell it as-is.

That thought made her pause. What if she could do a little more than spruce up the house? She'd always harbored a love of home-improvement shows. What if she could remodel it a bit? The inheritance she received from her mother sat in a savings account, gathering interest- she could use some of that if she budgeted carefully. Even small improvements could add a lot of value to a house. Some paint, new fixtures, maybe replace an appliance or two?

As for her job- her workload could easily be managed remotely for a couple of months, and there was usually a lull at the end of the year for the holidays. She could theoretically stay in Alaska until close to Christmas and no one at the office would miss her much.

She could make this happen. She was strong, smart, capable,

and not afraid of manual labor in the least. She had a good eye for interior decorating and had always dreamed of designing her own custom home one day. Why not try out remodeling a house that had been suddenly dropped in her lap?

What if she could flip this house and make enough money to build herself a forever home in the Seattle suburbs?

A plan began to formulate in Stefania's mind.

Step one: Pack.

Step two: Get to Alaska.

Step three: Assess the house.

Step four: Make a potentially life-altering decision.

Step five: Execute the potentially life-altering decision.

Step six: Be home by Christmas and start the new year with a clean slate.

That night when Stefania began packing, she packed her work laptop and a lot of extra clothes.

Just in case.

The security guard barely spared Stefania a glance as she walked through her office lobby on Monday morning. Her favorite guard, Gerald, had retired five months ago and his replacement was not nearly as friendly. She sighed inwardly at the thought of missing Gerald's smiling face and held her security badge up to the card reader.

It flashed red, then beeped once.

She tried again. One flash of red, one beep.

Two more tries yielded the same results. She resisted the urge to roll her eyes and turned back to the security desk, where the guard was pointedly ignoring her struggles. "Would you please check my badge? It doesn't seem to want to work for me today."

"Are you sure you're in the right building?"

She didn't deign to reply to that insulting remark and just handed over her badge. The guard muttered to himself and pecked out a few keys on the keyboard. "Did you get fired and just forgot?"

The urge to roll her eyes intensified. "Not that I'm aware."

He shrugged. "It wouldn't be the first time that's happened." After a few long minutes of hunting and pecking, the guard finally handed back over her badge. "I don't know how to fix this. I'll just let you in today."

Stefania stared at him. "What about the rest of the time?"

"The rest of the time?"

"Any other time I need to get back into the building?"

The guard shrugged again, clearly unbothered by her plight.

She took a deep breath. "Can I just get a new badge that works?"

"I don't know where those are kept. You'll have to come back in when Angel is working."

This was just getting better and better. It was like talking to an obstinate five-year-old. "When is Angel working?"

"I don't know. She's usually on the night shifts."

What DO you know? She wanted to shout at him. Just that moment, she was saved by another colleague walking out through the doors. Smiling gratefully at the beautiful blonde as she passed, Stefania slipped through the door and beelined to her cubicle. The badge issue could wait until she was back from Alaska- today, she was only here to grab her headset and a couple of files.

She approached her plain grey cubicle and stared down at it. In her youth, she had vehemently protested against the idea of an office job, often proclaiming that she didn't want to spend 40 hours a week in a box. But the need to be independent weighed heavily on her, and her current position allowed her to live comfortably by herself. She was thankful that being a graphic designer still allowed her to be creative and use her art degree.

She just wished she didn't feel so alone in this corporate hellscape. Since she'd been here, the number of people in the office that she actually liked to talk to had dwindled down to a select few. The rest of her department either now worked remotely or in different offices, and an influx of young, hip new-hires had made her feel every one of her thirty-seven years.

She was definitely looking forward to working remotely for the foreseeable future.

Headset and files obtained, she headed back out to the lobby. The security guard didn't look up from his phone as she passed.

Gerald had better be enjoying his retirement.

Chapter 2

Stefania

Stefania sighed with relief as she stepped out of the law offices of Platt, Platt, Platt, and Platt. Seriously, what were the chances of four siblings all going into law in Winterhaven? The snow-dusted town, while charmingly rustic and teeming with activity in the late Tuesday sunshine, couldn't have a population of more than 1,000 people. Perhaps such a small town lent itself to boredom, and thus enabled folks who had nothing better to do push the boundaries of the law.

Or... her overactive brain immediately jumped to the conclusion that the law firm *must* be a front for the mafia, as she didn't see how they could possibly stay in business otherwise.

There, it was settled. Mystery solved. She could move on.

The train had departed from Anchorage an hour late due to a mechanical error, but thankfully she had still arrived in Winterhaven in time to make her appointment. The consultation with the four lawyers had been gloriously brief, with the eldest

Platt commanding the meeting (potential mob boss? Stefania would need to ruminate on it or perhaps not read so many mafia romance novels, and it didn't help that they were *all* tall, dark, and handsome due to the miracle of genetics) and finishing it in record time. The will of Charles Clarke was read, the paperwork was signed, the keys to the cabin and a vehicle were handed over, and Stefania was hustled out the door back onto Main Street by the administrative assistant, whose voice she immediately recognized from last week's awkward phone call. She still didn't know the assistant's actual name.

According to the file folder she clutched in one hand, Stefania was now the owner of a parcel of land about twenty minutes east of Winterhaven. She was pleasantly surprised to hear that the northern property line ended at Denali State Park (not to be confused with Denali National Park, she learned), so at least some of the land would be protected from future development.

Denali itself loomed ever-present in the background of Winterhaven, providing a spectacular view of which Stefania didn't think she could ever tire. The view of the summit was clear of clouds at this particular moment, and she marveled at all 20,310 feet of the beautiful mountain (she'd looked it up) as she rolled her luggage down the brick sidewalk, which had thankfully been cleared of most of the snow. She still needed to figure out how to actually get to the property, and her earlier search for a rideshare had been in vain. No taxis or rideshare companies operated out here.

But first, food. Stefania hadn't eaten since leaving Seattle that morning and her stomach was starting to protest the lack of sustenance. She made a beeline towards the coffee shop she had spotted earlier about a block away from Platt, Platt, Platt, and Platt. Random folks waved at her as they passed her on the street, and she was forced to awkwardly flap the file folder at them in response. Everyone in Winterhaven seemed very friendly, with the exception to that rule being the long-suffering law firm assistant.

Stefania stepped through the door of the coffee shop (aptly named Beans, Beans, which Stefania surmised was due to the popular children's rhyme) and glanced around at the empty seating area. The shop closed in fifteen minutes according to the sign on the door, and she hoped that whoever prepared her food wouldn't spit in it for making them cook so near to closing.

A short, curvy woman with an angelic face and the most beautiful blonde hair Stefania had ever seen was behind the counter, wiping down the back of the display case. The woman's face lit up as she smiled, bright blue eyes roaming over Stefania and taking in the luggage she rolled behind her. "Hello there! Is this your first time here?"

"Hi," Stefania replied, sliding her luggage next to the counter and releasing it with a shake of her hand. She smiled back at the woman, who appeared bursting at the seams with good health and happiness. This woman was the sunshine trope personified. "Yes, first time in Winterhaven, actually. My great-uncle used to live here and I've come to sell his property." She figured gossip would travel quickly in a community like this, and maybe the property would sell faster if more people knew she was a motivated seller.

The woman's smile faded slightly. "Who is your great-uncle?"

"Charles Clarke," Stefania replied as she looked down at her luggage, concentrating on unzipping a pocket and stuffing the thick file inside. "He passed away recently. Did you happen to know him?" In a town this size, how could the woman *not* know him?

"Oh, Charlie!" The woman exclaimed, pressing a hand to her chest. The movement drew Stefania's attention to the name embroidered on her bright pink apron. Bridget. "He was such a dear. Didn't know him too well, as I've only been here a few years and he kept to himself. Really only came to town to sell his carvings over there at the Winterhaven Market." She pointed across the street to what appeared to be a general store. "But he was always nice to me whenever he stopped in for a coffee. Sad to hear that he had passed."

Stefania nodded her thanks. She wasn't sure how to prevent the conversation from turning awkward. Did she mention that she'd never met him, never even knew he existed until four days ago? Or just plow on, accept the sunshine and platitudes, and order food?

She opted for the latter and was soon crunching away on warm wrap filled with vegetables, hummus, and cheese while Bridget continued cleaning up and occasionally tossing out random Winterhaven facts to Stefania. Stefania soon learned that the Platt brothers had come to Winterhaven from New York (her mafia theory gained more ground in her head) and were famous in the area for successfully defending the town against a big oil corporation that had wanted to drill on the borders of Denali National Park (the mafia theory crumbled a bit). They'd had no shortage of clients since.

Mystery *actually* solved, she thought to herself.

She did notice that Bridget's voice got a little higher when she talked about the Platt brothers and was willing to bet she had a crush on one (or all) of them. She filed away that tidbit for later.

Stefania crumpled up her napkin when she was finished and stood to take her little paper basket to the recycling bin. Walking over to the counter, she asked, "Do you need any help cleaning up? I feel bad that you stayed late on account of me."

Bridget waved her away with the rag she was using to wipe down the counter. "Don't worry about it at all, you've been great company. I'd still be here cleaning anyways!"

Stefania glanced at the sky outside. It was starting to darken into dusk, and she was still without any way of getting to the property. She guessed that the temperature would also be dropping rapidly. It wasn't slated to snow this evening, but it would still be bitterly cold. "Are there any taxis in town? Any way to catch a ride or rent a car?"

"There aren't any taxis and the only place to get a rental car is at the dealership down the block, but I can guarantee that they've closed up for the evening. Almost the entire town rolls up the sidewalks early when the days are shorter." Bridget paused. "But I think Ana sometimes delivers groceries in the evenings, so you can check if you could ride along with her. I'd offer to take you, but I have to prep food for a catering gig tomorrow."

"Who's Ana?" Stefania asked.

Bridget pointed across the street again to the Winterhaven Market. "She runs the Market. Super sweet and would give you the shirt off her back, although you wouldn't want to make her mad. She's liable to hex you."

Stefania couldn't tell if she was joking. "Thanks, I'll give it a try. And thank you for feeding me and telling me a little about the town."

The curvy little blonde beamed at Stefania. "It was nice to meet you, Stefania. I hope to see you around here more." She winked. "Maybe permanently if you decide to fall in love with the place like I did."

Stefania stepped into the Winterhaven Market and admired the layout of the store. It had the homey appeal of a general store with its worn plank floors and rows of neatly stocked wooden shelves, which rose about five feet off the ground. The combination of the low shelves and wood beam ceilings gave the store an open, airy feel that Stefania immediately appreciated. As she walked further into the store, she noticed neat racks of clothes in the back corner next to a section marked "Local Vendors".

Remembering what Bridget had mentioned about Charles' carvings, she made her way over to the Local Vendors section. There were shelves filled with beautiful pottery, knitted clothing, sterling silver jewelry, small paintings, and *there*- on

13

two shelves at her waist level, stood rows upon rows of wooden figurines.

Stefania bent down to examine the unpainted carvings. She could tell right away that they were exquisite- she was blown away by the amount of detail each figurine possessed. The majority were animals she figured were common in Alaska, such as bears, wolves, and eagles, each one painstakingly carved with intricate whorls of fur or spiky feathers. They were so *lifelike*, as if they would spring off the shelf at any moment.

A larger figurine towards the back of the shelf caught her eye and she reached in to pick it up, delicately weaving it over the tops of the others. It was different from the rest as it was not an animal and was more abstract in style. It lacked the intricate details within its smooth shape, but was still beautiful in its simplicity.

She turned it this way and that in her hands. It appeared to be two humanoid figures, consisting of a curvy female shape and a slightly bulkier masculine shape wrapped around each other in an embrace. Stefania glanced at the base for the price ($60.00) and found a small artist's mark and the words "The Hug" scratched neatly into the surface of the bottom.

She stared at the piece in her hands. *The Hug*. It was invoking emotions in her that she was not prepared to deal with today. When was the last time she had enjoyed such intimacy? Yes, some of her acquaintances hugged her when they saw her, but it was not the same as a loving embrace shared with a partner. Stefania was a strong, independent woman, but physical touch was one of her love languages and she had been starved for it ever since Doug the Drag. Doug had resisted any attempts at cuddling in the beginning of their relationship, claiming it was too uncomfortable for him and he got too hot. Eventually, she'd given up even trying.

"That piece is a one of a kind," a voice near her said, snapping her out of her reverie with a jolt. She almost dropped the figurine but caught it and held against her chest. "The artist died recently and I think that's the only one like that he ever made."

Stefania turned to see a gorgeous woman with bright blue and purple hair standing next to her. She was as tall as Stefania, with striking light green eyes highlighted by bold eyeshadow and colorful tattoos that ran up her arms and disappeared under the short sleeved black dress she was wearing. The woman smiled, and Stefania noted that she had a metal ring pierced through the center of her full lower lip, glinting against her metallic green lipstick. "Can I help you with anything?"

Stefania cradled the figurine protectively against her chest. The animals were beautiful, but *The Hug* elicited such an emotional response from her that she knew she couldn't leave without it. It was a stark reminder of what she was wanted in life- affection, love, an equal partnership. She deserved it. "Actually, yes! I need to speak to Ana- I'm hoping to catch a ride to my great-uncle's cabin. I just got in today, the rental place is closed, and Bridget mentioned that Ana might be able to give me a ride."

The woman's grin widened. "I'm Ana. Who is your great-uncle?"

Stefania glanced down at the figurine she was still clutching. "Charles Clarke."

"Ah, I'm very sorry for your loss," Ana said as she looked over the rows of figurines on the shelves, her bright expression fading. "I delivered groceries for him often in the past few months as his health deteriorated. I can drop you off, not a problem at all."

Stefania breathed a sigh of relief. "I'd really appreciate it- thank you. How can I pay you?"

Ana waved her off, several rings sparkling in the lights of the store as she moved. "No payment necessary, I'm going in that direction anyways. The store closes in about thirty minutes- why don't you grab some groceries for your stay in the meantime?" She eyed Stefania's thin coat and luggage. "You

15

might also want something a little thicker than that jacket, trust me. Gloves and thick socks too, if you don't have them."

"Thanks," Stefania replied. "I don't know how long I'll be here, but I think I'll take that advice just in case."

Ana's smile reappeared as she turned towards the front of the store, flipping her blue and purple hair over a shoulder and revealing an ear studded with jewelry. "Let me know if you need anything else- I'll be at the register."

Stefania's gaze followed Ana as she walked away, and her eyes caught on the knee-high iridescent shit-kicker platform boots the woman was wearing, which had to be adding at least five inches to her height. *She must be a pro at navigating icy sidewalks in those,* Stefania thought to herself with no small amount of envy as she turned back to the shelves of carvings.

Chapter 3

Stefania

The drive to her great-uncle's land was slightly harrowing in the dark, as Stefania soon found out. Ana navigated the narrow roads with expert ease, occasionally pointing out entrances to different unmarked hiking paths off the side of the road. Stefania tried to catalog all of it in her mind- an exercise in futility as it was so dark all she really saw were the snowbanks piled beside the roads from the plow. She'd drive back this way when it was daylight and do some more exploring.

If she had time for it. She had to stick to her list and complete steps 3-4: *Assess the house. Make a potentially life-altering decision.*

Along the route, Stefania and Ana had fallen into easy conversation. Ana told Stefania what she knew about Charles, which unfortunately didn't seem to be any more than Bridget had relayed. Charles mainly kept to himself, was kind to everyone, and had come to the Market at least once a month to bring a fresh supply of carvings to sell. In all the times Ana had dropped groceries off at his house, she had never once gone inside. A note had always been included in the online order: *Knock and leave deliveries at front door.* Ana figured Charles must have enlisted a caretaker or a friend to handle the unloading of the groceries, but she had never seen another car in the driveway on any of her visits.

In turn, Stefania had opened up a little about the circumstances of her visit. Ana listened to all of it with a sympathetic ear and offered up condolences again for the situation. Stefania was finding that she quite enjoyed Ana's company- she was easy to talk to and satisfyingly blunt when it was called for. Ana didn't know any reason as to why Charles had never tried to contact Stefania- by all accounts, he had been a kind, affable man.

About fifteen minutes into the trip, they turned off the main road onto a gravel drive that was covered by a few inches of snow. Would the driveway would need to be plowed if a storm rolled through? She wasn't sure what she needed to do to make that happen- just another addition to the list of things to research. The trees crowded the sides of the road and gave the impression of leaning over the car, making Stefania feel a little claustrophobic. "This is a little creepy," she noted, craning her head towards the windshield to get a better view of the snowy branches.

Ana laughed, maneuvering her car through the snow with ease. "The cabin is about a mile down this road. The view is beautiful when the sun's out, I promise. Although, it's absolutely gorgeous at night when the aurora is active."

"Do I need to be worried about bears?" Stefania asked, turning to look at Ana. The idea of seeing the northern lights was very exciting, but she was a little anxious about encountering the local wildlife while trying to get a glimpse of the aurora. Her condo in Seattle didn't have many threatening creatures except for random seagull invasions.

Ana chuckled again. "Yes, and the occasional moose. Don't drive down this road fast, I've spotted them on it before. They're a lot bigger than you think they are. Don't hike without some sort of spray- even though it's getting colder, some of the bears may still be active. Don't leave anything on your porch at all. I think your uncle paid for garbage pickup, so there is probably a special locked bin for you to put your trash in."

Ana continued on, and Stefania tried to absorb the information to the best of her ability. She'd be safe from people since Winterhaven was a small community and crime was virtually non-existent. According to Ana, the threats all came from nature- the predators and especially the cold. "And mosquitoes," Ana cheerfully commented. "They thrive for a few months in the summer and it's miserable for us humans. They're basically the bloodthirsty state bird of Alaska."

Stefania didn't bother reminding Ana that she had plans to be out of Alaska by Christmas at the latest, long before mosquito season. "Anything else I need to be worried about?"

"If you're really wanting to sell the place, you'll probably hear from Gary Klein once he catches wind of you. He's one of the two real estate agents in this town and he's a bit of a jerk."

Stefania glanced at Ana and noted that she was suddenly white-knuckling the steering wheel. "He's a jerk? What does he do?"

Ana sighed. "He's a misogynist asshole and a classic gaslighter. Nothing is ever his fault. He has a tendency to talk over women and doesn't listen to a word they say. And I would know- I dated him for three months." Ana sighed again and continued to explain. "The dating pool around here is very shallow, and I was feeling particularly lonely when he asked me out. It's been a long time since we've dated but I know he hasn't changed one bit."

Stefania didn't hide her cringe at the idea of working with such a person. "Please tell me there's someone better I can work with."

Ana nodded. "I'll get you a card for Kim, the other agent in town. She'd be happy to help you sell... and she will actually listen to you. But I selfishly hope you stick around."

Stefania managed to thank Ana just as they rounded a final curve in the road and the cabin came into view.

At first glance, Stefania could see that the home was a mid-sized log cabin with a wraparound porch and an attached two-car garage. She couldn't see much of the snow-covered yard in the light of the car's headlamps, but she did spot a large metal container off the side of the house that she supposed was the garbage bin. She'd have to wait for more daylight tomorrow to explore the outside of the cabin.

Ana pulled up in front of the garage door. "Charles' pride and joy is in there- a 1973 Ford F-150. Drove it to town every week until he got too sick." She laughed. "I only know the year and model because he mentioned it to me a few times- he bought it brand new in the seventies, and was very proud of it."

Stefania stared at the garage as she got out of the car, her shoes crunching in the snow. The will had mentioned the vintage truck, but she didn't know what she was going to do with it. At over fifty years old, she imagined it was a rust bucket and she'd be lucky if it even ran. "Do you know if he has any other cars? The will only had one listed on it."

"He probably has a snowmobile in there, those are common up here. You can take it into town if you really bundle up." Ana unloaded the luggage from the trunk and put it next to the porch steps. "Are you okay? I can come in and help you unload if you want."

Stefania collected the grocery bags and smiled over at Ana. "You've done enough already- thank you for driving me out here. I owe you lunch at some point this week!"

Ana waved the comment away as she shut the trunk and walked over to the driver's side door. "While I'm not worried about payment, I will take you up on the offer of lunch. It's been nice to talk to another person close to my age. Besides Bridget and me, there aren't too many of us around here. Let me know if you need any help, all right?" She pointed to the grocery bags Stefania had in her hand. "There's a card with my phone number on it in the bag with the cheese."

Ana waited in the car while Stefania climbed the porch and fumbled with the ring of keys the law firm had given her. She was thankful for the headlights of the car providing much-needed illumination as she finally found the correct key and slid it into the deadbolt. She opened the front door and slapped around on the inside wall, trying to locate a light switch. The house should still have electricity- the Platt lawyers mentioned that all of the bills would automatically pull from Charles' bank account until Stefania turned off the utilities.

She hadn't yet had the chance to look over the paperwork detailing how much money had been left in his accounts or what bills she would need to manage. She was exhausted and would look into it tomorrow.

Tonight, she would take a look at the house, hopefully find some clean sheets to put on a bed, shower, and collapse into said bed.

Her hand hit a switch and a light flickered on inside the house. She turned and waved to Ana, who saluted cheekily in acknowledgment and drove slowly back down the driveway. Stefania stood on the porch and watched until the red from the taillights was swallowed by the inky blackness of the surrounding trees. She shivered as she realized just how pitch black this forest was. She was no stranger to dark woods, having solo camped in a few places over the Pacific Northwest since her split with Doug, but there had always been *some* type of light pollution. Not here.

Once Stefania got her luggage and groceries inside the front door, she finally allowed herself a look at the cabin interior. She was standing in a large, open living room with a vaulted ceiling, the light from the overhead fixture illuminating the space. A massive freestanding wood stove sat towards the back of the room, a neat stack of firewood next to it. An oversized, comfortable-looking leather sectional couch with a coffee table in front of it was in the middle of the room, angled slightly towards an old box TV she could see on the left wall. She eyed the TV- it looked positively ancient and she wondered if her great-uncle even had cable out here. Definitely not getting a high-definition picture on that old screen. *At least the couch looks like it was purchased within the last decade,* she thought.

She continued her initial inspection of the house, exploring each of the rooms in turn. The living room appeared to be the heart of the home, with a guest room and office on one side and a main suite on the other. The kitchen and dining room were in the back, separated from the living room by the wood stove. The majority of flooring consisted of wide wooden planks that looked worn with foot traffic, but she was willing to bet a good sanding and refinishing might bring them back to life. She added that as another item on the mental list.

Her eyes drank in more details of the cabin as she explored, noting with relief that most of the furniture appeared to be loved and clean, if a little shabby. She had half expected the house to be a mess and covered in cobwebs, but everything was neat and spotless as if someone had come and deep cleaned the house for the next occupant, and she was eternally grateful to whomever had completed such a task. There were no dishes in the sink, no trash in the bin under the sink (she was thankful to not have the house smelling like old garbage), no dust bunnies rolling over the worn rugs scattered throughout the house. Her earlier thought about Charles having a caretaker must've been correct.

She could see evidence of Charles' woodcarving talents everywhere. Multiple small figurines were placed on surfaces throughout the cabin, and Stefania felt a little silly that she'd bought the wooden statue at the Market only to bring it back to its place of inception.

Ana had tried to give the artwork to Stefania, claiming that most of the money would only go back into Charles' account anyway, but Stefania had insisted she pay for it on principle. She might take one or two of the animal figurines with her when she returned to Seattle, but *The Hug* was the one piece she wanted to feel like was hers. She still didn't see any other carvings that even remotely resembled the entwined figures.

Charles's talents evidently hadn't stopped at figurines, as she noticed that each of the door frames had delicate scroll-work carved into them. Swirls and whorls had been carefully extricated from the wood of each corner, adding a little extra personality to the mostly bare plank walls.

She realized that despite the wealth of carvings on display, she found no evidence of a woodshop or tools of any kind. *It all must be out in the garage, or he got rid of it all when he got sick.*

Charles had obviously been a gifted artist and she felt a small connection over their shared artistic ability spark to life within her chest.

Somehow though, it made her feel even more alone.

Why did he never contact me if he clearly knew I existed?

She was pleasantly surprised to discover that the main bathroom had been recently renovated as it boasted heated tile floors, a massive shower next to an equally impressive freestanding tub, and a toilet that appeared to have a heated seat and a bidet built into it. A floor-to-ceiling window with retractable blinds stretched along one of the walls, and if she hadn't been in the middle of absolutely nowhere, she would've second-guessed that design choice. There wasn't anyone around for miles, though, and she highly doubted that her great-uncle had any creepers trying to catch a glimpse of him as he showered.

The shower itself was downright heavenly and she instantly fell in love with it. It appeared to be built as a roll-in shower with plenty of space for a wheelchair to maneuver. It didn't have a door or a curtain, just a 3/4 wall of glass that separated it from the rest of the bathroom. The fixture was rainfall-style and mounted into the ceiling, far enough away from the shower entrance that the any water spray would be easily contained. A bench sat along the back wall, with a detachable shower head close by for accessibility. She hadn't noticed any evidence of a wheelchair in the house, but perhaps Charles had been preparing for that possibility when the shower had been installed.

She'd seen a similar shower design before in magazines, but had never stepped foot in one. Having now seen such a shower in person, she vowed to put the same design in her dream house along with a soaking tub big enough for three people- exactly like the one in the corner. She'd probably never leave the house if her bathroom back in Seattle was like this one.

Stefania sighed with relief as she returned to the living room, her mini-inspection complete. She'd have to wait until the morning to check out the garage and the outside of the cabin, but the interior of the house was in good condition. A good polishing, some updated kitchen appliances, and some elbow grease was all it seemed to need. Barring any massive exterior renovations or unforeseen incidents, she was confident that she'd be able to make her Christmas deadline.

But at this precise moment, she was going to enjoy that luxurious shower.

Chapter 4

Oswald

Oswald peered around the tree he was hiding behind, trying to get a better view of the interior of the cabin. He had been curled up contentedly on the mattress in his small hunting shack when he heard the car approaching in the distance and came to investigate. Oswald didn't think there was anything of major value in the house, but potential thieves wouldn't know that.

Charles had been good to him, and the least he could do was to protect the property of his late friend.

He had reached the cabin right as the car was pulling back down the driveway, too late to see who it was. Instead, he watched as a figure opened the door and wrestled multiple bags into the house. Surely this wasn't a thief- they would *take* things rather than *bring* things inside.

He observed the house from his vantage point for a while, taking note as lights turned on in each of the rooms for a few minutes, only to switch back off as the person inside moved on. Whoever was in the cabin was in no hurry. Was this someone from the bank? Or maybe the law office Charles had mentioned?

Charles had known his health was declining and had gone to the Platt firm to settle his affairs, although he had not disclosed any of his plans to Oswald. He had simply patted Oswald on his paw and said "You'll be fine, I'm making sure of it."

That had not been very comforting.

Oswald knew he could relocate if he needed to. He was a yeti, and therefore had thick white fur that kept him safe from the Arctic elements and camouflaged in the snow. He could easily hunt and sleep outside or find a nice cave to stay in, but he had to admit that he had enjoyed the stability, relative warmth, and indoor plumbing of the little cabin Charles had gifted to him years ago. He would prefer to stay if given the option.

Most yeti-folk managed to live their whole lives without being discovered by humans, as it was vital for their survival to remain hidden. However, most yeti-folk also lived in the Himalayas and had far less of a chance of being accidentally spotted.

His parents, long since gone, had trekked from the Himalayas when his mother became pregnant with Oswald. They had been dreamers and adventurers, wanting to experience the world outside of their small clan. Their exploration had taken them across the top of the world to Alaska, eventually settling near Denali several years after Oswald's birth.

Unfortunately they passed away right before Oswald reached his age of maturity, falling in a deep crevasse while on a family expedition up the steep mountain slopes. Oswald had been downslope from his parents and watched in horror as they fell, unable to do anything as they disappeared below the snow and ice.

Rather than return to the Himalayas to live with the yeti clans, Oswald had opted to stay in Alaska. It was his home, after all, and he did not know how he would fit in with the clan- he knew he was as different from the other yeti-folk as his parents had been. How would he, an outsider, fare amongst the tight-knit clans?

So he had remained, resigned to be alone in the wilderness.

His run-in with a human had definitely been unplanned and changed the course of Oswald's life. Shortly after his parents' deaths, Oswald had been hunting in the forest when he walked through an old bear trap, buried and forgotten from years ago. The rusted trap had snapped shut around his right leg in a tight vice, cutting through fur and flesh in an instant.

Charles had heard Oswald's initial yowl of pain from his cabin and brought his shotgun into the woods, prepared to put some poor creature out of its misery. Oswald could still remember the look of utter shock when Charles came into the clearing and spotted the gangly young yeti. Oswald knew enough about human hunters to know that guns usually were bad news for wildlife, and he had closed his eyes and lay in acceptance of the inevitable.

He would either be killed immediately or trotted out in front of the world as a freak of nature.

It was unfathomable, but Charles instead carefully freed him from the trap, murmuring calming words the entire time in the foreign tongue of the Alaskan humans. Oswald lay there as still as a stone, too frightened to move and cause more pain in his leg and terrified of this human who could so easily end his life. Yeti-folk were taught to avoid humans at all costs as they could be cruel to that which they did not understand, but Oswald was soon in too much pain and sorrow to care much if he lived or died.

Charles, though... Charles had been different. It was Charles who strapped the young yeti to his snowmobile sled and drove him back to the cabin, soothing Oswald's scared grunts all the while. It was Charles who patiently cleaned his wound and patched him up, keeping him there through the worst of winter while he recovered. It was Charles that slowly taught him English, although having fangs made Oswald speak it with a slight lisp.

And it was Charles who had given him something to do during recovery and sparked his interest in a new hobby. Charles noticed the yeti gouging small designs in the bed frame with his claws, so he bought Oswald a small woodworking kit, complete with tools and patterns. Oswald had immediately taken to the art form (although it took some modification for him to hold the tools with his big furry paws and long black claws), and was soon producing small figurines to show his appreciation for his rescuer.

After a few months, Charles had suggested selling the little carvings to earn some money for Oswald, although Oswald thought he had no use for it. He was a yeti- what was he possibly going to buy? He had instead insisted that Charles keep it and use it, as thanks for everything he had done.

Years went by and they settled into a comfortable friendship. Charles gave Oswald one of the small hunting cabins on his property, outfitted as much as possible to accommodate Oswald's newly filled out yeti body. As Charles' health declined the past year, Oswald had stayed with him in the main cabin to take care of him as much as possible. He had nursed his friend to the best of his ability, filled with sorrow to see him succumb to his illness.

Charles had slipped away peacefully in his sleep over two weeks ago. Oswald had cleaned up the cabin, called the hospital from the cabin's landline phone, then left before the first responders arrived. He hadn't returned since.

And now... now some stranger was in the cabin of his only friend.

Oswald, now confident that the strange human wasn't paying attention to what was outside the windows, slowly crept closer towards the front porch. He'd need to disguise the tracks on his way home, but at the moment he was too engrossed in his investigation to take the time.

He was nearing the steps of the front porch when it hit him.

The *scent.*

The scent.

He staggered back a few steps in the snow and slapped a paw over his heart as the delicious smell of berries and vanilla invaded his nostrils and short-circuited his brain.

He felt like he couldn't breathe, couldn't see, couldn't think.

It was a human woman- he could tell that much from the sweet scent. In the past, Oswald had smelled a variety of humans on Charles when he returned from town (including the faint undertone he could now detect of the shopkeeper who used to deliver food), but *the new one...* this woman's scent was intoxicating.

A primal urge he'd never felt before shot through him like lightning through his veins. He *needed* to see this woman immediately. He was going to go absolutely feral if he couldn't lay eyes on her after smelling her incredible scent. He stumbled hastily around the cabin, clawing his way around the side of the house where the main bedroom and bath were. He'd just get a glimpse and then he'd go cover his tracks and resume his watch from the tree line and everything would be *fine-*

He stopped cold when he reached the corner of the bathroom window.

There she was- the woman he scented.

Naked.

Bathing in the massive shower stall Charles had built in the anticipation of his mobility loss.

Oswald's brain short-circuited further as all the blood instantly rushed south to another part of his body.

Her back was turned to him. Oswald pressed his face to the window, unable to stop himself. She was utterly perfect with her long legs, voluptuous curves, and pale skin dotted with freckles like constellations. Her wet auburn hair flowed down to her waist and drew his attention to the curves of her ass. He imagined holding that beautiful round ass in his paws as he pounded into her from behind-

A low rumbling noise began in Oswald's chest. He stepped back from the window and slapped a paw over his heart again, but it didn't do anything to stop the sounds emanating from his chest.

A voice in the back of his brain told him to leave. It was too much to take- he had to tear himself away somehow before the urge to break through the window and *ravish* this woman became unbearable. He'd gotten the glimpse he wanted and now he was staring at her naked, glistening body, his cock unsheathed and growing harder and harder by the second. He should go. He *should*.

And then she turned around in the shower, eyes closed and arms stretched over her head, massaging her scalp.

Oswald felt like his skin was on fire beneath his fur as his eyes drank in the sight of her. He'd only ever seen the naked female form in the few art books Charles had procured for him and occasionally on the television, but in the flesh? Nothing compared to this. She was the most gorgeous work of art he'd ever seen, with ample breasts and a nipped-in waist decorated with a flower tattoo, flaring out into generous hips and leading to strong thighs that he wanted to bury himself between and stay there for all eternity.

She tipped her head up under the spray of water and he tracked the water droplets as they fell across her beautiful face and down the graceful column of her neck. Tendrils of her red hair plastered to her shoulders and Oswald wanted to gather it all up in his claws and hold it in a fist while he rutted her.

An involuntary shudder wracked through Oswald, making him almost drop to his knees. He dimly realized that he was unconsciously stroking his cock with one paw, the rumbling in his chest growing even louder with the movement. A low whine escaped from his throat.

Her eyes snapped open.

He tore himself away from the window, fumbling through the snow towards the woods. The vibrations in his chest stopped abruptly as the instinct to run took over. Had she seen him? He thought he'd been fast enough to avoid those eyes that he now knew were a captivating deep green like the pine trees in his forest, but he couldn't be sure. He'd been too close, too reckless, and now he was paying the price as he held his aching groin in one paw and flung himself through the trees.

He needed to go back to his cabin. *Now.*

Oswald stumbled into his cabin and slammed the door behind him, chest heaving as he panted wildly. He wasn't entirely sure how he'd made it back here, sprinting blindly through the thick woods as his brain (and his cock) entirely focused on the beautiful woman he'd just seen. He'd never had such a visceral reaction to anyone else- but her scent, her curves, her long, long legs with those thighs- he was obsessed. Utterly obsessed.

His cock jerked, thick and throbbing with need. He stroked a paw down the length and noticed that even the knot at the base of his cock had swelled, which had never happened before in his life. He was no stranger to pleasuring himself, but yeti knots had a purely instinctual function and only swelled when a male spotted a potential mate.

As he'd been either by himself or with Charles since his maturity, Oswald had never encountered a creature that had piqued that primal interest.

Thoughts of the bewitching stranger swirled through his head and he stroked himself again, a guttural growl ripping its way out of his throat. He had to relieve some of this pressure so he could think clearly again and figure out what to do. He *needed* to know more about her, to know what she was doing in Charles' house, to know why she was the cause of such undiluted, uncontrollable lust.

Oswald spit on his paw and began to shuttle it up and down his cock, rotating his wrist and squeezing as he reached the tip. He leaned his back against the front door, not caring that he was about to spill all over his living room floor. He couldn't physically make it to his usual spot in the shower- if he didn't touch himself now, he was sure to go insane and tear all the fur off his body.

He closed his eyes and pictured her here in the cabin with him, her gorgeous naked body splayed on his bed while he feasted between her thighs. Her berries and vanilla scent still filled his nostrils and he imagined how she'd taste, how she'd moan, how she'd writhe...

Release began to gather in his lower spine. His fantasy morphed into flashes of the two of them in various positions and he worked himself faster and faster with each vision.

Her hands replacing his as she stroked him off.

His black claws making indents in her hips while he rutted her from behind.

Her big breasts bouncing in his face as she rode his cock.

When he couldn't take anymore, he fisted his knot in his other paw and squeezed hard, driven by instinct. His eyes wrenched open and he bellowed as sheer pleasure barreled through him, stealing away his ability to stand and dropping him to his knees. His release- more than he had ever thought possible- spilled out onto the floor in a seemingly endless stream of thick ropes.

Panting heavily, Oswald leaned back on his heels and rested his head against the door. Small aftershocks pulsed through his body as he slowly uncurled his paws from himself. He'd made a mess of himself and his floor.

Utterly drained, he didn't care one bit.

He knew deep down in his soul that he'd never be fully satisfied again until he could bury his knot within that exquisite woman and claim her as his.

Chapter 5

Stefania

Stefania woke up the day after her arrival feeling refreshed. She had slept in the main bedroom after finding that the only other mattress was a double bed in a guest bedroom. A few long white hairs were stuck to the comforter of that bed, and she wondered if Charles had a dog. There was no other evidence of a pet- no water bowl, no leash, no food bag anywhere- so she assumed it must've been adopted after his death or it, too, had recently passed.

After last night's initial perusal of the house, she had showered in the giant shower stall, changed the sheets on the king-sized mattress, and promptly fell into a deep sleep. Today, she would inspect the cabin in greater detail and compile a list of everything she wanted to do to the house.

She was eager to explore the outside of the house in the daylight. So far, the house seemed solidly built. She didn't feel any cold drafts, hear any creaking floorboards, or see any wayward critters skittering across the floor, all of which were a win in her book.

Stefania made quick work of preparing her coffee and breakfast, after which she bundled up to go into the snowy yard. No fresh snow had fallen last night, though the sky was beginning to fill with ominous grey clouds. She mentally thanked Ana for the advice regarding the warmer clothing and tugged on her new scarf, gloves, and fuzzy hat. She hadn't arrived totally unprepared for the bitter November weather, but she admitted that the Alaska wilderness was a whole other level of cold and she was glad for the extra layers.

She stepped onto the front porch and gazed out into the yard, a notebook and pen poised in her hands for copious amounts of note-taking. Weak sunlight glittered off of the snow and she took in a deep breath to enjoy the fresh pine scent that emanated from the forest surrounding the cabin.

It's really very lovely here.

While she took stock of the layout of the yard, she noticed furrows gouged into the snow off to the side of the porch. The spacing of the divots resembled relatively fresh animal tracks- the bears she had been warned about, perhaps? She continued down the steps and found the clearest print to examine.

Stefania wasn't well-versed in animal tracks, but this didn't look like a typical bear paw. The imprint seemed much bigger and almost human-shaped except for the five deep gouges at the top of the print, obviously made by long claws. Maybe there were mutant bears in Alaska or a different species that she didn't know about?

She snapped a photo with her phone so she could run a reverse image search on it later. Much to her dismay, there was barely any cell signal here. She'd found a wi-fi router last night, but was unable to locate the password to log on- yet another item on her to-do list. Surely it was written down and stuffed in a drawer *somewhere.*

The tracks continued around the side of the house and stopped in front of the bathroom window before veering off directly into the thick woods. Stefania had a flashback of her shower last night- she thought she had opened her eyes at one point to see two eyes as blue as glacier water staring back at her, but she blinked and they had been gone. She'd chalked it up to a hallucination due to exhaustion, but perhaps she'd seen the mutant bear.

Hopefully it was long gone and wouldn't be back.

She continued her examination of the outside of the home and soon had a page full of notes on potential improvements she could make. There were some easy fixes such as a new paint job for the porch and a new back door, as well as some more labor-intensive issues like the insulation falling down in the crawl space. She could handle the smaller tasks, but she would need to hire someone to fix the insulation. She considered herself a capable, self-reliant woman, but every person had their limits. Crawling under a house and dealing with fiberglass insulation was one of hers.

She'd get a professional out here to see if she had missed any major problems, but she was satisfied that the cabin was in great shape overall and wouldn't fall to pieces the second she tried to sell it. The garage thankfully seemed to be in the same good condition. After a thorough inspection of the outside, she pressed the button to open the main door, bracing herself for whatever pile of rust she would find inside.

There was no pile of rust.

Instead, Stefania beheld a shiny black vintage truck, obviously well-loved by Charles. A few specks of dust were scattered here and there, but they did nothing to sully the flawless paint job. Peering through the window, she could see that the interior was immaculately clean with spotless black carpet, a shiny black dashboard, and a grey cloth bench seat that stretched across the length of the cab. Her heart stuttered a bit as her eyes roved across the truck, now understanding Ana's comment about the truck being Charles' pride and joy. She'd dismissed it as a small joke when she'd heard that the truck was a 1973 model, expecting it to be a venerable piece of junk.

She silently chided herself for jumping to such unfair conclusions.

Seeing this beautiful truck, this worn but well-kept house... it made her even more determined to figure out what sort of person Charles had been. He was obviously someone who took great care of his beloved belongings.

The ancient snowmobile parked next to the truck looked like it had seen better days, but the truck...she ran a hand over the hood, admiring the flecks of silver in the black paint.

"Isn't it a great truck?"

Stefania bit back a scream and whirled around. Standing a few feet away was a tall, lean man with salt-and-pepper hair and a sheepish smile on his face, one hand tucked away in the pocket of a paint-splattered work jacket.

"I didn't mean to scare you, miss! My electric car doesn't make much noise, especially when muffled by snow. I'm Henry Ciraba, an old friend of Charles. You must be his great-niece? I heard from Ana that you had come to town. Came by to say hello." He gestured to the truck, his smile growing into a grin. "Tried to get him to leave me that truck in his will, but he insisted that it go to you."

Stefania willed her pounding heart to calm and stuck out her hand. "Hi Henry, I'm Stefania Clarke. It's nice to meet you."

Henry took her hand in a firm but gentle grip, his calluses scraping across her skin. "It's nice to meet you, too. I can see the family resemblance- you both have the same eyes. And that red hair! His was white for the past twenty or so years but it started out the same shade as yours."

She unconsciously put a hand to the braid that snaked its way out from the bottom of the fuzzy hat. She hadn't started digging through any of Charles' personal effects, so she'd seen no pictures of his younger years, if they existed at all. The man had been a mystery so far.

"You knew him for a long time, then?"

Henry nodded, patting the side of the garage with fondness.

"Ever since I came to Winterhaven with my husband about thirty years ago. Charles hired me to help build this house- I'm a contractor. Well, a semi-retired contractor these days." He shrugged ruefully. "The cold makes the arthritis in my hands act up and it's hard to work. Now I mostly just boss around the younger crews at my company."

Stefania gestured to the house. "Would you like to come in? I have so many questions about Charles." She was desperate for any information she could glean, and surely an old friend like Henry could help solve the mystery.

Henry nodded again and held out an arm for her to lead the way. "I wouldn't mind a cup of coffee if you have any, but then I have to run to a job site. I'll be happy to answer as many questions as I can."

As they neared the front door, he spotted the animal tracks in the snow and Stefania watched as surprise flashed across his features. It only lasted an instant before the easy smile returned to his face. She pointed to the tracks. "I'm guessing a bear came by last night, although that paw imprint doesn't look like any bear paw I've ever seen. I think it's too big to be any kind of cat and it's definitely not a moose. Do you know what it could be?"

Henry waved dismissively as they climbed the porch steps. "Bear tracks can be in all shapes and sizes. I wouldn't worry too much about it, just keep your trash locked up. They'll start hibernating any time now."

She didn't miss how he took one last quick look at the tracks before heading inside.

Stefania handed Henry a steaming cup of coffee and sat across from him at the kitchen table. Where to even start with all of the questions that were bubbling up inside her? She supposed she should just rip the proverbial bandage off and ask her most burning questions.

She drew in a deep breath to steady herself.

"Do you know why Charles never contacted me or my

mother? Or why I've never heard of him?"

Henry cupped his mug in both hands and sat back in his chair, glancing down at the table where Stefania had placed *The Hug* statue as a centerpiece. "Charles was... a complicated soul. We didn't talk much about his life before he came to Winterhaven. I asked him early on in our friendship if he had any family that he would be visiting during the holidays and the answer was no. His tone was so forceful that I took the hint and didn't pry any further. My husband and I had him over for Thanksgiving every year after that."

Stefania took a sip of her coffee. "So, you have no idea why he isolated himself from the rest of the family? There has to be some reason!"

Henry hedged for a few seconds, staring at the mug in his hands. "I don't know any of the details, but one day after a few glasses of whiskey, he alluded to an accident in his youth that resulted in the death of someone he loved. It seems he blamed himself, but whether or not it actually was his fault, I have no idea. But after the accident, he became a deep-sea fisherman for a few decades before retiring and settling down in Winterhaven." He heaved a sigh. "I think... I think his isolation was a form of self-punishment. If he couldn't get close to anyone else, then he couldn't hurt them, or be hurt in return."

Stefania let that information sink in for a moment before replying. "That's a long time to punish oneself. He never mentioned any details about the accident? Nothing at all?"

Henry shook his head. "I was a few glasses deep myself that night and apparently, I'm a terrible investigator when alcohol is involved. It never came up in conversation again- I think he realized what he'd revealed and locked those memories away. Charles was an extremely private person about his past."

"Do you know how he found me?"

"I do know the answer to this one," Henry replied. "When he got sick, he wanted to get his affairs in order, so he hired the Platt firm to see if his brother- your grandfather, I take it- was still alive. When they found out he had passed shortly after your mother was born, they traced the family records down to you. I tried to tell Charles to reach out to you, but again, he was stubborn. He didn't want to burden you with a dying old man."

Stefania swallowed a lump in her throat. "He wouldn't have been a burden. It would've been nice to know that I had some family after all." She swallowed again and looked out the window towards the forest as she fought through the sudden pain in her chest. She would've been overjoyed to have a family connection, however fleeting, after being lonely for so long. "Can you... can you tell me what he was like?"

Henry smiled, his eyes crinkling at the corners. "He was smart as hell- beat me in backgammon almost every time we played. He was a good man, and a kind one, though he kept almost everyone at arm's length. I knew him for over thirty years and I couldn't tell you what truly went on in his head."

He paused to take a generous gulp of coffee, and Stefania took the moment to gesture at *The Hug* sculpture.

"Most of his carvings are of animals, so he must've loved them. This piece, though- it isn't like anything else I've seen of his so far. Do you know anything about it? What motivated him to carve it?"

She was desperate for any detail she could glean about the beautiful piece of art.

Henry looked down again at the entwined statue and cleared his throat, his face going a little pale. "Yes... he loved animals. A great artist. Very talented." He stood abruptly. "Thank you for the coffee, but I've got to go."

He fished a business card out of his wallet and handed it to Stefania. "Here's my number. If you have anything you'd like done around the house, please let me know- I know this cabin inside and out. I tried to get Charles to make more updates to this house for years but he insisted that everything still ran perfectly. I was hoping the bathroom remodel we did last year would've sparked his interest in changing a few other things, but he was stubborn as a mule... and then he got sick before I could hound him any further."

With that, he waved goodbye, let himself out the back door, and disappeared down the ramp.

Stefania was a little taken aback by his sudden departure, but she supposed asking about the statue had hit a nerve for Henry. He had just lost one of his dearest friends, and here she was grilling him with all these questions.

I'll apologize the next time I see him. But can you blame me for wanting more information about my mysterious long-lost relative?

Disappointment filtered through her as she moved to the living room window to watch Henry's car silently slip back down the driveway. It was beginning to look like Charles was an introverted loner who kept all of his proverbial cards close to his chest. Had anyone ever really known him?

Speaking of which... she studied the card in her hand that had Henry's phone number and company name (Ciraba Contracting) embossed in bold black letters. Henry showing up out of the blue had multiple benefits- she'd learned a little more about Charles and made a valuable contact for her renovations. Once the repair list was finalized, she'd call him and get him back out to the cabin for a quote.

First item on her current list, though: finding the wi-fi password.

Chapter 6

Oswald

Days passed, and Oswald spent each one in the woods outside of the main cabin, hoping for glimpses of the mystery woman. *His* mystery woman, because there was no doubt in his mind that she had the potential to be his mate. Every morning at sunrise he trudged to the house and hid nearby, watching her every movement throughout the day.

He only returned to his small cabin at night to relieve the pressure of his cock, except for one snowy night that he'd been unable to stop from stroking himself, hidden in the tree line as he watched her shower. He came with a roar that shook the snow loose from the trees and she'd pressed her face to the bathroom window, trying to see what animal had made the noise. He'd scuttled away, feeling embarrassed and achingly unfulfilled.

This feeling, this utter *obsession* he had with this woman- he didn't know what to do about it. He only knew in his bones- in his very soul- that he needed to see her, needed to be close to her. Her scent remained the sweetest thing he'd ever smelled, and every time she stepped outside of the cabin, he had to restrain himself from snatching her up, carrying her into the woods, and rutting her senseless.

These primitive urges shocked Oswald as he was normally a calm, rational yeti, but something about her drove him absolutely wild.

He still didn't know her name. By now he realized that she must be a relative of Charles and had inherited the house upon his death, and each day he watched construction crews and delivery drivers come and go from the cabin. His chest had rumbled with jealousy and a compulsion to *protect, protect, protect* his woman, but he suppressed the feral urges and remained hidden.

Nothing good would come of him rushing into the cabin and scaring all of the humans, including her. He knew rationally that he should hold no thoughts of actually revealing himself to her and no hope of her ever consenting to be claimed as his, but *if* they should ever meet, he did not want to take the chance of terrifying her on their very first encounter.

But every time he caught a whiff of her scent, heard the faint sound of her laughter, or managed to spot her beautiful face through the trees, it got harder and harder for him to stay away.

She left the property a few times, taking Charles' black pickup truck into town and returning a few hours later with supplies. He'd been tempted to follow her in the truck- he was big and fast and could've kept up if he'd sprinted, but good sense had won out and he'd moped in the forest instead, idly whittling twigs down to nubs with his claws or hunting whatever small game he could find. Getting close to the town meant a bigger chance of being discovered and he couldn't risk it in the daylight, even though it grated heavily on his nerves to let her out of his sight.

Was she safe? Would she even come back? Or worse- would she be interested in the human males in town? Would she invite one back to the cabin?

His jaw clenched so tight at this thought that his molars ached and his fangs threatened to pierce his lip.

His head was a mess.

He recognized that he needed to soothe the primal beast that now stalked beneath his fur, but none of his usual habits seemed to calm his racing thoughts. No amount of brushing his fur or whittling sticks or jerking himself had any effect at taming his raging emotions.

Deep down, his beastly inner urges were screaming to be set free.

He wasn't sure how he long he could continue along this path before he would need to remove himself from the situation altogether, and even thinking about leaving made him growl in frustration. This was his home and he wanted to stay and protect her, but at what point did he need to protect her from himself?

Almost two weeks had passed by when Oswald realized how he could channel his chaotic thoughts into something productive. His work was nonexistent since she'd burst into his life and he hadn't made any new figurines or etchings. The majority of his time had been consumed with watching her every move.

He needed to carve.

More importantly, he needed to carve something for *her*.

Even though he'd grown up far away from the clans, his parents made sure he was somewhat well-versed in yeti culture, including their courtship rituals. As a young yetling he'd understood that he would probably be the sole yeti in this region and wouldn't ever court another unless he returned to the Himalayas, and thus hadn't paid too much attention to those particular lessons. He resigned himself to a life of solitude and had been at peace with that decision until *she* had dropped into his life.

As far as he remembered, the courtship rituals were fairly simple. The yeti would leave small gifts at the mouth of the cave of their intended, such as tools, small decorations, or food. If the yeti being courted brought the first gift into their cave, then the courtship was accepted and the suitor was free to leave more gifts. This went on daily for an undetermined amount of time, until the courted yeti was satisfied with the commitment of the suitor and ready to complete the courtship.

Some yeti-folk held out for more presents, making their suitor leave gifts for weeks or months until they considered themselves won over. In the case of Oswald's parents, that first gift was all it took for his mother to immediately accept the courtship and mating of his father. When they first relayed this story to their son, Oswald imagined that that the gift must've been something extremely elaborate in order to make his mother fall in love so fast.

In reality, the token had been a small, plain rock that his father had etched their names into with a claw. At the time, Oswald had thought it silly that his mother had accepted so simple a gift. But as the years went by, he realized that his mother had already loved his father unconditionally and hadn't needed nor wanted anything fancy.

To finalize the union of yeti-folk matings, one final mating present was bestowed from the suitor to their mate. It was a time-honored tradition amongst the yeti, given during a small ceremony in which each of them pledged their hearts to the other. Yeti-folk were simple creatures, but they loved fiercely and usually mated for life.

A picture began to take shape in Oswald's mind.

He would begin his courtship of this woman the only way he knew how- by initializing contact with a gift.

The human woman probably would not appreciate having dead animals dropped upon her doorstep, so he chose another option: his carvings. There were many small ready-made figurines laying around his cabin, but those had not been carved with anyone in particular in mind, just an appreciation of each individual animal. No, he needed to pour his heart out into this first offering, making something she couldn't resist even if she didn't know it came a yeti- a species of monster in the eyes of most humans.

While he was at it, he would start working on the mating present. The chances of him being able to present her with the mating gift at a ceremony was nonexistent, but it settled his mind to have some sort of plan in place to work off this frenetic energy.

Oswald returned to his tools and got to work, carving deep into the night.

The next day before the sun rose in the sky, he prowled onto the porch of Charles' cabin and dropped a small bundle on the front stoop. He carefully covered his tracks and returned to his usual hiding spot in the forest to wait.

And wait.

And wait.

She never came out the front door that day. Instead, she remained cloistered inside while Oswald paced back and forth through the woods, about to rip the horns out of his head in frustration. He spent the day circling the cabin, trying to peer into the windows from afar to see what she was up to.

He had no luck.

All the blinds, including those built into the bathroom window, were shut the entire day, and Oswald had to stop himself from kicking the door down and making sure she was alive and well.

Had the gift been rejected?

Had she seen him somehow? Had he not been careful enough in his delivery?

Was she holed up in the house to avoid him and wait for reinforcements to arrive?

When the stars twinkled high in the night sky, Oswald crumpled into a dejected heap against a tree, exhausted and feeling rather sorry for himself. The rational side of his brain scolded himself for making such a big deal out of this. What did he realistically think was going to happen- that she see the gift and immediately fall in love with the anonymous benefactor? She was a human, he was a yeti- where could this possibly go?

Chapter 7

Stefania

Stefania rolled over in the bed and cracked open an eyelid, searching for the bedside clock. She groaned when she saw that the time was 9:27am, which meant the contractors would be arriving any minute. She'd have to drag herself out of bed to let them in.

Yesterday had been a total wash- she'd woken up with an ocular migraine, unable to see much of anything but vague shapes and the squiggly patterns of the aura she always got during these episodes. She had scrolled blindly through her phone to call Henry and cancel for the day and instead accidentally video-called her ex-fiancé Doug on the first attempt. She'd hung up on him after mumbling that she couldn't see her phone properly, too loopy to be too embarrassed. Doug had never believed her when she told him how badly her vision was compromised when one of these migraines hit, just one more red flag she had brushed aside early on in the relationship.

She cracked open the other eyelid and was happy to discover that the aura was gone and she was able to see clearly again. She sat up carefully, still feeling a bit like she'd been hit by a truck. The migraine hangover was a very real thing and the rest of the day would need to be spent taking it easy. There was a small project she needed to complete for her work (as she had been working out of the cabin for the last week after finally locating the wi-fi password, inexplicably taped to the bottom of the utensil drawer), but after that, she could rest some more. At least it was Friday.

But for now, she needed to get up and unlock the front door for Henry and his crew. She couldn't afford to cancel another day of construction with the temperature dropping more and more as each day passed. With the added stress of fewer hours of daylight, the window for making any improvements on the outside of the house was rapidly closing.

She shuffled slowly to the front door, unlocking it and opening it just in time to see Henry on the front porch, holding a small parcel wrapped in old newspaper.

"Good morning, Stefania!" he exclaimed. Stefania winced at the volume of his voice and he had the grace to look contrite. "I'm sorry, dear. Are you still feeling poorly?"

"It'll take me another day to fully get over it, but I'm better than I was," Stefania replied. She glanced to the edge of the trees in the front yard, where she thought she'd heard a low, sharp growl. Nothing appeared to be out there, so she continued on, refocusing on the contractor. "I'll be fine. I need to catch up on some of my work today anyways."

Just then, she noticed a man standing behind Henry, one that she'd never seen before. He was short and stout, with black wide-rimmed glasses and a full grey beard hiding most of his face. His eyes, though, sparkled with happiness and crinkled at the corners in amusement. He beamed at her and stuck out his hand. "I'm Ben, Henry's husband and personal interior stylist. It's so nice to meet you, Miss Stefania!"

Stefania liked him instantly. She shook his hand and returned his warm smile. "It's nice to meet you, too." She glanced down at her pajamas, a matching top and pants with a black and gold celestial pattern printed on them- her softest pair that wouldn't trigger any sensory overload as she recovered from her migraine. She crossed an arm over her chest, trying to look inconspicuous about hiding the fact that she wasn't wearing a bra. *I doubt these two care, but it's cold out here and I'm about ready to cut glass with these!* "I'm sorry that I'm not better dressed, I just woke up. What brings you out here today?"

Ben's smile widened, showcasing a set of perfect white teeth under all that beard. "Henry has been talking about you and this cabin for two weeks now, and I wanted to come up and have a look for myself. Plus," he added, holding up a large thermos, "I brought you some of our homemade butternut squash soup. Henry mentioned you weren't feeling well, so I thought this might perk you up. Always works wonders for us!"

Henry took this moment to hand her the little package he was holding, and she reluctantly moved the arm that was covering her chest to take the box. "Found this on your doormat! Amazon must be saving on packaging these days. That paper looks like it's from the fifties at least."

Stefania stared at the old newspaper wrapping, turning the package over. "I haven't been expecting anything until tomorrow, so I'm not sure what this is." She stepped to the side of the door and waved Henry and Ben into the house. "Please come on in out of the cold. The soup sounds wonderful, thank you!"

Henry turned and gave a thumbs-up to his construction crew to get started for the day before stepping inside. "They're going to finish up work on the garage today, and then we'll replace some of those boards on the front porch. I'll make sure to tell them to work as quietly as they can. They won't do anything in here today so you can concentrate on feeling better."

Stefania expressed her thanks and padded towards the kitchen, placing the package on the counter to open later. "If the porch could get done today, that would be wonderful- Ana and

Bridget said they'd help me make some raised flower beds in front of it tomorrow. Can I get you two anything? Coffee? Tea?"

Ben shook his head as he followed her into the room and handed her the thermos of soup. "Oh no, my dear. We're not going to stay- you need your peace and quiet." He linked his arm through the crook of Henry's elbow, gazing fondly at his husband. "Henry's going to give me a quick tour to show me all the things he's done so I can properly *ooh* and *ahh* over them, then we'll get out of your hair."

Henry mirrored the adoring look towards his husband, then turned his attention back to Stefania. "We also want to invite you over for Thanksgiving next week! No pressure to attend, but if you feel up to human company, you're always welcome at our house."

Stefania's chest ached a bit. She envied the casual intimacy and obvious love that these two shared. "Thanks, Henry, I'll think about it and let you know."

Henry grinned at her before shepherding his husband out of the kitchen, calling out, "Your new appliances are coming on Monday- I wouldn't blame you if you want to stay home and test them out!"

The two men made a quick circuit around the cabin, with Henry quietly pointing out the improvements Stefania had ordered and Ben dutifully fulfilling his obligation to *ooh* and *ahh* over them. Thus far, she was very pleased with how the cabin was coming along and was thrilled to continue to mark things off of her list. The floors had been thoroughly cleaned and buffed to a shine, all the light fixtures had been replaced, and the guest bathrooms had been freshened up with new vanities and toilets. A new washer and dryer had also been installed in the small laundry room, replacing Charles' sturdy but ancient machines.

Not too shabby for a couple of weeks' worth of work, she thought. Henry's team had a reputation for quality work done at a fast pace, and it was well earned.

Her goal was still to get the house on the market in time for Christmas, and there was no doubt in her mind that the crew would meet the deadline and exceed her expectations while doing so. The ever-present list of tasks was checked daily to make sure everything was on track. A few curveballs had been thrown her way that required some adjustments to the plan, but the majority of the house projects were coming along fine.

Her old kitchen appliances would be swapped out on Monday as Henry had mentioned, but she was going to have to wait for the first week of December for work to begin on the rest of the space. Though old, the kitchen cabinets were still beautiful and in great condition, so Stefania opted to preserve them and simply swap out the hardware herself. New counters and the addition of a nice tile backsplash would complement the new stainless-steel oven, dishwasher, and refrigerator she had ordered.

She shuddered to think of the expense that was going into this renovation, but each receipt was faithfully logged and she was determined to stretch the budget as much as she could. After settling in Winterhaven, she had visited the bank and found that Charles had left her a moderate sum of money, almost all of which she funneled back into the house. From her initial design discussions with Henry, Stefania believed that's what Charles would've wanted- for someone to put a little love into the house and cherish it as he had.

I'll cherish it for the short time that I have it, while I get it ready for the next owner.

This week she'd also begun sorting through Charles' personal effects, of which there were very little. Charles, it seemed, had been very prepared for his death and purged all unnecessary items from the house, a fact that she was simultaneously thankful for and saddened by. She had spent an entire evening poring through a few photo albums she'd found that included pictures of her grandparents, a very dapper young Charles (later color pictures from the 70's revealed that he *did* have the redhead genes), and a handful of black-and-white photos of Charles with a beautiful young woman whose name didn't appear to be mentioned anywhere. Who was she? A sister? A cousin, a friend, a lover?

Stefania had scoured the back of the photos that featured the young woman, hoping for a name to be written somewhere. No luck.

What she did find, much to her surprise, was an envelope full of cash with the words *FOR OSWALD* scrawled across the front of it, tucked away in the bottom of a desk drawer. There were several thousand dollars in the envelope and Stefania had set it back in the drawer, just in case this mysterious Oswald came to her door looking for the money.

She briefly entertained the thought that maybe Charles had been indebted to the mafia (perhaps the Platt brothers) and this Oswald was a collector, fated to show up soon and demand the money. She, being a strong, independent woman, would demand receipts and steadfastly refuse to give him a penny more than what was owed, causing her to gain Oswald's grudging respect and unabashed lust. Oswald was a good strong name, she decided, that must belong to a good (or at least morally grey) strong man.

She *really* had to stop reading so many steamy mafia romances.

There would be no reading today, though, as she would have a hard enough time staring at her computer screen for work. Stefania popped the migraine medicine under her tongue to dissolve and tried not to gag at the faux-peppermint taste. *Why can't medicine taste like bacon or chocolate?*

Her eyes landed on the little package that Henry had brought inside and she picked it up, turning it over to examine it from all sides. There was no shipping label attached to it, so it definitely had not been delivered by a package service. Did one of the construction crew arrive early and put it on her doorstep? That didn't seem to be plausible- Henry's crew was professional and respectful towards her and she didn't think she had any secret admirers amongst them. Was it something that had been uncovered it in the yard or hidden somewhere in the garage?

She carefully peeled away the yellowed newspaper wrapping (*from 1961*, she noted wryly), uncovering a small wooden box that fit neatly in her palm. Though slightly rustic in its construction, it was absolutely gorgeous. The lid and all four sides were covered in an intricately carved swirling motif, with tiny flowers- *lilies*- dotted throughout the pattern. The attention to detail in every swirl and flower was stunning- someone had obviously devoted a lot of time and energy into this carving.

Running her fingers over the smooth etchings, she turned the box over and looked at the bottom, noticing that it bore the same maker's mark as her *Hug* statue. One of Charles' designs, then- someone on Henry's crew must've found it.

She opened the box to reveal the interior, which only contained a single etching spanning the width of the bottom. It was another lily; this one was more embellished than the small ones on the outside of the box. It was simply exquisite.

A pang of sadness radiated through her chest, aching at the fact that she never got to meet Charles. How sad it was that talent such as his was no longer present in the world. *Had he just learned of my mother's name when he made this box? The wood smells so fresh, like he just finished it yesterday.*

Stefania padded to the main bedroom. The box could live on the dresser for now- it would make a good place to store her rings and her favorite necklace until she decided what to do with it. She might keep it. The lilies were a direct reminder of her mother, and she could pretend that Charles had carved it in honor of the niece he had never met.

She ran a hand absently along the right side of her ribcage, thinking of the beautiful watercolor lily tattoo she had gotten after Lily's death, so her mother would always be with her. The design of the lily on the box was shockingly similar to her tattoo.

Perhaps this was a sign from the universe or from Charles

himself that the box was meant as a gift for her.

She wasn't sure what to do with the other carvings left behind. She wanted to keep some to honor his memory, but what about the rest of them? The idea of pocketing any posthumous profit from Charles' works of art made her feel uncomfortable and slightly icky. Perhaps the carvings could be donated to schools or assisted living homes, or even distributed among the residents of Winterhaven? All of the pieces were beautiful and she couldn't fathom anyone turning them down.

She added another item to her never-ending list: *Pick Bridget and Ana's brains regarding carving donations.*

Stefania leaned the rake against the front steps and surveyed her handiwork. Ana stood beside her, wiping a tattooed forearm across her sweaty brow, while Bridget shucked off her gloves and gathered her blonde hair back from where it had escaped from her messy bun. The trio had worked all morning, using stacked stone pavers to create flower beds that flanked the porch. A few hardy shrubs had been planted for curb appeal, but they had left plenty of room for new flowers to be planted in the spring.

Bridget blew out a breath as she finished fixing her hair. "I am *beat*. But look at what we've done!"

Ana grinned and gave her a high-five. "Teamwork makes the dream work, baby!"

Stefania smiled over at them both, incredibly grateful to have made friends like them in this tiny town. Ana and Bridget both cheerfully worked alongside her the entire day, never once complaining. *Well, except one or two complaints from a certain blonde about a certain Platt brother being impossible.* Stefania's smile widened at the thought. There was *definitely* some palpable tension between the tiny baker and the handsome brooding lawyer, and her smut-loving brain was dying to know the details.

Though Ana and Bridget seemed like total opposites at first

glance (the tattooed goth girl and the epitome of bubbly blonde sunshine), they were fast friends and had quickly adopted Stefania into their group. Both of them possessed hearts of gold and Stefania felt a sharp twinge of sadness at the thought of leaving them when she returned to Seattle.

Not caring that they all smelled like potting soil and sweat, she gathered them both into a hug. "I can't thank you enough. These look great!"

Ana grinned at her as they parted. "I like doing this kind of thing, it's always good karma and gardening is fun anyways. And I like being useful to my friends. After all, what's your favorite ship?"

Stefania's brows crinkled in confusion. *Favorite ship?* "Um... the Millennium Falcon?"

Bridget's petite curvy frame shook with mirth as she sputtered out, "No, silly... *friend*ship!"

Stefania threw her head back and laughed. "I've never heard that before. Well, that's now my new favorite toast, thank you for that!"

Ana glanced at her watch, her giggles trailing off. "Oh, I hate to cut and run, but I need to head back to the store to do some inventory tonight."

Bridget raised her phone screen to check the time. "I've got to go as well, I have to do some prep-work for Monday. Everyone will be coming into Beans to stock up on baked goods for the storm. I'll come on by Monday afternoon and bring you some, if you like!"

"I'll bring you some blizzard essentials as well, just in case. Maybe copies of some of the smuttiest romance novels I have in stock?" Ana wiggled her eyebrows suggestively.

Stefania groaned in appreciation. "You two are the literal *best*. Baked treats and smut? You're going to spoil me!"

Ana grinned wickedly. "Maybe we're just trying to convince you to stay in Winterhaven."

"Add in some cheese and there's a good chance I'll never

leave," Stefania replied, shrugging. "It doesn't take much to make me happy!"

Ana and Bridget departed, leaving Stefania to admire the front of the house on her own. She admitted to herself that the cabin was adorable and the flower beds looked amazing against the front porch. A large hammock hanging in the corner of that front porch would be perfect to lounge in and read on rainy days. Or maybe one of those swings that were as big as a bed, covered in cozy cushions and pillows, primed for ultimate relaxation in pre-mosquito springtime weather?

She frowned. Maybe she would talk to Henry about installing some mesh screening in a part of the porch as protection from the swarms of the bloodsuckers. *Then again,* she thought, *I won't be here next mosquito season, so the next owner can figure that out.*

Stefania climbed up the stairs and sat on the top step next to a box of Christmas lights that Ana had brought over. Ana was determined to bring some holiday cheer to the cabin and blatantly ignored Stefania's protests that she'd be gone by Christmas. "Christmas basically starts after Halloween up here," Ana had replied. Bridget had immediately backed her up, claiming, "You'll want some happy lights on your house when it's dark almost all the darn time."

Stefania had given up and accepted the box of lights.

She ran a hand through the box of neatly separated coils. *Maybe I'll put up one dinky little strand just to try and satisfy them both.*

She stared out at the dense forest encircling the house, taking a few moments to appreciate her surroundings. It was so peaceful here. The oftentimes harsh, overwhelming noises of Seattle life were nowhere to be found here- only the gentle ambient sounds of nature.

With a start, she realized she didn't miss Seattle at all. There had been no bouts of homesickness or any desire to return to her small apartment, and she was definitely more suited for remote work. She'd be perfectly happy if she never saw that odious office security guard ever again.

Though tired from the hard work of building the flower beds, Stefania felt the sudden urge to explore the woods. There were a couple of hours until dark and the weather was relatively warm for late November. She had been a Winterhaven resident for over three weeks and she was itching for the chance to check out the marked trails on the property.

Trails- on her own land! *That* had been a fun discovery, made when she uncovered a sketch of the various tiny hunting cabins around the area. There were a few separate trailheads leading away from the cabin in different directions, all of them seemingly large enough to fit a small snowmobile or four-wheeler. However, if the condition of the paths were terrible, any machines would get stuck and she'd be stranded out there. She'd be much more nimble on foot.

The prospect of checking out more of the beautiful Alaskan scenery was too good to pass up, and Stefania went inside to arm herself with a light jacket with a zip pocket for her phone, a bottle of water, and a small pocketknife. She'd been working so hard- she could spare an afternoon to go for a quick jaunt in the forest.

It was time to pick a trail and see where it took her.

This property is absolutely gorgeous, Stefania mused as she wandered through the snowy forest, keeping close to the marked trees as she took in the Alaskan wilderness. Each step cemented her earlier thoughts about how much she enjoyed the peace up here. And having a large piece of land of your own to hike on? Simply amazing. Her introverted side loved it- no air pollution, no fighting the crowds of people on popular trails... *I should've done this weeks ago.*

Her mind wandered as she walked, conjuring up a fantasy of what living in Winterhaven could be like. Cozy movie nights with Ana and Bridget. Lazy afternoons spent reading on a hammock on the porch or by a crackling fire. The yard had plenty of room for a nice fire pit- she could envision herself wrapped up in a plaid flannel blanket, roasting marshmallows under the stars.

Maybe a Platt brother could visit every once in a while, when she felt like having the company of a man- just not Bridget's Platt brother.

After what felt like a couple of miles, Stefania found herself on the bank of a rapidly flowing river that wound its way through the landscape. She vaguely remembered seeing this river on the sketched map of the property layout, with a long ribbon of water crossing through the top right edge of Charles' land.

Her mother Lily would be pleased. She had always said that when buying property, you should make sure it has running water on it in case of emergencies. Or in case of zombies, since they couldn't cross rushing water (according to the TV shows).

No zombies here, thankfully.

She gazed at the river, admiring the beauty of the water sparkling in the late afternoon sun. This part of the river was shallow. Giant rocks jutted up out of the water, stretching across the entire span to the other side. They were spaced close enough together that a person could hop across if they were careful. A trail marker was posted on a tree on the far riverbank, but a glance at her watch told her that she had already gone too far for today. She would come back when she had more daylight and continue along the trail.

Stefania turned away from the river, preparing to follow her own footsteps- and immediately froze, breath catching in her throat as a chill radiated down her spine.

Oh…my…gods and goddesses…

A brown bear stood in the path about thirty yards from her, sniffing her tracks in the snow.

It was utterly massive- the size of a hatchback car, she figured, with paws twice the size of her head. Its back was currently to her, nose to the ground as it snuffled her footprints. It hadn't yet seen her through the trees.

A small miracle.

She'd never been this terrified in her life. Her hands started to shake while her brain screamed at her to *move, move, move! Get away before it spots you!*

Her thoughts raced as she stood stock-still. Did she try to escape or try to stay hidden? Were they similar to the dinosaurs in Jurassic Park that only saw prey when it moved? Climbing one of these massive trees wasn't an option and would be a fruitless endeavor if the bear decided to climb up after her.

Why didn't I listen to Ana and bring bear spray?

Making up her mind in a split second, she slowly pivoted back to the river while keeping one eye on the bear. Dusk was falling and she couldn't afford to wait and see if it lumbered away. She would cross the river and follow it until she found another spot to cross back over. She had no idea if such a spot existed or if it would be as easy as this rock bridge, but she'd cross that metaphorical (but hopefully physical) bridge when she got to it.

First step was to escape immediate danger of the bear. The rest seemed like a cakewalk, especially if she had enough signal on her phone to use the GPS.

She didn't have much of a choice- she had to try.

And so she went.

Stefania leaped from rock to rock, trying to be as quiet as possible to avoid alerting the bear to her presence. Just a few more rocks and she'd be on the other side, hopefully safe and sound.

Five more steps.

Four more steps.

Three mo-

Stefania slipped on a slick rock and tumbled into the water, the shock of the fall ripping a small scream from her mouth as she went down. The ice-cold current immediately swept her downstream,

It was cold- so cold. And so *fast*. The water was deeper than she had anticipated, and she flailed through the rapids, desperately trying to get her bearings. All thoughts of the brown bear vanished as her body was pulled downstream, scraping mercilessly against rocks.

Fuck, fuck, fuck! Get to the side of the river! Shit!

She fought to keep her head above water, gasping as her hands and feet scrabbled for purchase against the slippery rocks of the river bed. It was too cold to focus, too cold to get a breath in, too cold to feel her hands. Was this it? Was this how she left the world, in the middle of the forest where no one knew where she was? Would she wash up miles downstream or just be lost forever to the Alaskan wilds?

She could dimly hear the bear over the noise of her frantic thrashing as it pounded along the river bank behind her, the sound of breaking branches echoing through the woods. She'd momentarily forgotten about the big creature, and reality instantly swept back in.

She wouldn't wash up downstream.

She'd be eaten.

There would be no body to discover, as she would become bear food.

She was granted no further time to contemplate it. Her torso slammed into a boulder, temporarily stunning her and knocking what little breath she had gulped in back out of her lungs. The force of the impact spun her around and she careened headfirst down the river. She gasped for air as she attempted to paddle her arms, desperately trying to right herself in the water.

The current was too fast.

Trees and rocks zipped by in her limited field of vision, the sounds of growls and snapping twigs growing closer and closer. The bear must be very near if she could hear it over the roar of the rushing rapids.

She caught a glimpse of a blurry white shape running

towards her through the trees. *Is that a wolf? Shit!*

No time to think about another predator- she was panicking and quickly losing strength. She was so *cold*. She needed to focus and find a calm eddy in the river before her body shut down. There had to be one somewhere soon, or a bend in the river, or-

Pain suddenly blossomed in her skull and she stopped fighting the current, too stunned to move.

Tiny dots swirled in her vision.

Everything began to go hazy.

This is it. No, no, no!

An ear-splitting roar was the last thing Stefania registered before she blacked out.

Chapter 8

Oswald

Oswald's heart seized painfully in his chest as he frantically clawed his way across the river towards Stefania.

Stefania. A beautiful name for a beautiful woman- it suited her.

He had finally learned it yesterday morning, overhearing it from his vantage point in the woods as he waited for her to accept the courting present he'd left on the porch before dawn. An accidental growl of pleasure had slipped past his fangs when the sound of her name hit his ears, and he'd held his breath when she had turned in the doorway to look in his direction.

A small part of him ached for her to see him.

And then, she had taken the gift inside. According to yeti-folk customs, the courtship had been accepted and he was free to continue to leave her presents. The joy he felt could hardly be contained, but it swiftly turned to anxiety as the day wore on. What was her reaction to the box? Did she like it? Was it too elaborate? Not elaborate enough? What if she didn't like carvings or the material and required something fancier? What if he'd freaked her out because he etched the lily using her tattoo design as inspiration?

He needed to content himself with being her secret admirer, forever watching from the shadows.

But now his beautiful mate- for she *was* his mate, he knew it in his bones- was in danger, forcing him out of the shadows and into the frigid, swirling river. He'd been only steps away when he'd seen her head bounce off of a rock, her body falling limp and eyes closing within seconds. The water around her began to bloom red with blood.

Another roar, this one laced with agony, shook itself from his chest as he finally reached her. Her pale face was above water, a fact for which Oswald briefly thanked the universe as he gathered up her sodden form in his arms. Cradling her to his chest, he picked his way over to the river bank, his big body spearing through the river on powerful legs. He was built for the desolate peaks of the Himalayan mountains, so the freezing cold water barely affected him.

Not like his poor mate.

He knelt on the river bank and kept her as close to his warmth as he could, supporting her with one arm while his other paw gently checked her over. She was still breathing, her chest rising and falling with each shallow breath passing through her blue-tinged lips. Blood trickled from the wound on the top of her head and she shivered uncontrollably. He needed to get her safe, needed to get her warm.

Where?

They were too far away from the main house, but he could sprint to his little hunting cabin in a matter of minutes. He had no choice- it would have to do.

Oswald stilled as a movement to his right caught his eye.

A brown bear was approaching the pair cautiously, curiosity shining through its eyes. This must've been what Stefania had been running from when she fell into the river- Oswald had been shadowing her from afar and hadn't seen why she had crossed the river in such a hurry. The sound of her scream when she tumbled in still echoed in his ears.

The bear continued lumbering forward, sniffing the air.

Oswald's lips peeled back from his fangs in a sneer as he instinctively hovered over his unconscious female. "MINE!" he bellowed at the bear, every ounce of anxiety and rage and fear cracking through the word. He felt Stefania shiver and stir under him, but her eyes remained shut. "MINE!"

The bear stopped in its tracks and cocked its head at the pair of them.

Oswald gathered Stefania in his arms and stood, rising to his full height. He didn't have time to waste, he needed to get these sodden clothes off of her immediately. She was so cold, he felt like he was holding a block of ice in shape of a woman. "MINE!" he barked again.

Apparently his brain had short-circuited with adrenaline and reduced his vocabulary down to one word.

The bear took a step backwards, clearly debating on whether this massive white creature was worth the trouble. Oswald took a breath and channeled every ounce of dominance he possessed as he let loose a massive roar deep from his chest. "MIIIIIIINE!"

The woman in his arms didn't even flinch.

The bear got the hint and loped away, and Oswald spun on a heel and dashed back through the woods. He didn't need a map or trail markers to find his way around, having spent many years hunting through this forest. He sprinted in the direction of his cabin, taking care to not jostle Stefania for fear of injuring her more.

He didn't know what she'd do if she woke up in the arms of a monster- she'd probably scream and thrash and try to run from him, and the thought that potential rejection made his heart ache in his ribcage alongside his burning lungs.

He tucked his chin down and kept running.

Oswald kicked open the door of his cabin and stumbled inside, making a beeline for his little bathroom. The cabin- more of a well-maintained shack, really- was ridiculously small for someone of his stature as it had been built to accommodate one average human hunter, not a massive adult yeti. There was a sleeping area, a small bathroom, and an even tinier kitchenette. He would've been just fine living in the wilderness as he had in his youth, but he had to admit that he enjoyed the luxury of a hot shower. The little cabin suited Oswald's needs perfectly.

Unlimited access to electricity and running water was definitely a privilege he savored.

He gently set Stefania on the bathroom counter and leaned her against the corner of the wall, propping her head up as much as he could. She hadn't stirred once on his mad dash, and he was growing more and more concerned that she wouldn't wake up. Humans were so fragile, with their furless bodies and thin skin. She was so *helpless* compared to him.

He set the water in the shower to warm up and began to work on stripping off her freezing wet clothes. His big paws and black claws proved problematic, though, as everything besides the jacket was skin-tight and clung to her body. He winced as he sliced through the laces of her boots with the tip of a sharp claw, hoping she'd forgive him later. He peeled the boots off and managed to remove her socks, but it was taking too long.

Every second he was delayed in getting her under the warm spray of the shower felt like an eternity.

Enough of this.

With a growl of frustration, he carefully shredded the rest of her soaked clothing. He'd apologize to her on his knees later- right now, he *had* to get her body temperature back up.

Oswald didn't give himself any time to focus on her luscious figure as he peeled off the tattered remains of her clothing and scooped her off the counter.

He climbed into the shower, hugging her to him as he stood under the spray and let water wash over them both in the cramped space. He knew from listening to Charles talk about

65

humans and hypothermia (a totally foreign concept to a yeti) that the lukewarm water would feel like she was being doused in lava, but he held her close and stood firm. He'd stand there for hours as long as it saved her, even if it meant inflicting pain onto her.

Long minutes passed.

Eventually her shivering began to subside and her eyelids began to flutter, her face contorted into an expression of agony as the heat from the water registered on her skin. "I know, I know," Oswald murmured into her auburn hair. "I'm sorry."

He closed his eyes and inhaled a deep whiff of her berries and vanilla scent, willing his racing pulse to slow. She'd be okay- he had gotten to her in time. A whimper escaped her lips, the sound sending a bolt of anguish directly into Oswald's heart. "I know it hurts, but it'll help."

"Pain," she mumbled, her hands coming up to weakly clutch the fur on Oswald's chest. She tucked her head against his collarbone, her eyes still shut tight in agony. "Hurts."

Oswald spared a glance at her naked body. His anxiety, though still running at a high level, had calmed enough for his cock to start noticing the petal-soft skin and alluring curves nestled against him, and he mentally willed it to stand down. Now was not the time. He shouldn't be thinking about those perfect breasts mere inches from his claws, nor the apex of her thighs or the swell of her ass.

"It will be over soon." His fangs made it difficult to shape the sounds of some of the letters in the English language, and he tried to speak slower to enunciate better. "I will take care of you, I promise."

She clung to him, moaning, and his chest swelled at the feeling of her hands in his fur. When he'd deemed her warm enough, he turned off the shower and set her back on the counter, drying her off as gently as possible with one of his enormous bath towels. (Another gift from Charles. Yeti-folk were obsessed with cleanliness- it was so difficult to keep white fur in pristine condition.) Color had returned to her skin and the shaking had all but slowed to an occasional tremor. He propped her back against the wall, then stepped back in the shower and shook as much water as he could out of his fur, returning to her side to towel off any excess.

He then checked her for injuries, gingerly rotating various body parts this way and that to examine all her limbs. Oswald was relieved to see that the head wound had stopped bleeding and didn't seem to require stitches. Besides a myriad of small bruises and lacerations peppering her arms and legs, she had a big bruise on her ribcage on the opposite side of her lily tattoo.

He'd noticed that tattoo while watching her shower, and seeing it up close made him want to bend down and trace the delicate lines with his tongue.

She groaned again, and Oswald silently scolded himself for his inappropriate intrusive thoughts. She was injured and here he was, thinking with his cock, which was dangerously close to unsheathing itself. But he couldn't help but take a quick second to admire her lush body up close before carefully wrapping her in a dry towel- even covered in angry bruises, she was magnificent.

He dabbed a bit of wound care ointment on her scalp (it was pure luck that he had some) and then lightly scooped her up again in his arms. Her eyelids briefly fluttered open as he lifted her into the air and he froze, dreading her reaction.

One of her small hands drifted to his jaw as he held utterly still. Her fingers sifted through his facial fur before dropping back down, her eyes closing once more.

He could've sworn she whispered, "So soft."

Breaking out of his trance, he moved swiftly towards the mattress in the main room and laid her down on it with infinite care. A spark of fierce possessiveness shot through him at the sight of his mate in his bed, and he once again suppressed the growing lust with a low growl.

He had Charles to thank for even having a bed and clean

sheets in this cabin. When Oswald had first moved out here, he insisted that he didn't need any sort of fancy furniture. In fact, he would've been just fine on the floor like most yeti-folk, but Charles had balked at the idea. A simple but comfortable mattress had been purchased, along with several sets of sheets that Charles insisted he swap out for clean linens on a weekly basis.

Oswald had mentally rolled his eyes at the idea of a yeti needing anything as fancy as that, but he had learned quickly in the early days that Charles was stubborn and it was often pointless to resist when he set his mind to something.

But now, Oswald was grateful to have the sheets on his bed as he tucked Stefania under the covers. Never in his life had he imagined he would have someone like her in his home, much less in his bed. He carefully lowered himself next to her, angling the both of them so he could fold himself around her body as much as he could, trying to keep her as warm as possible. She fit perfectly against him, her head tucked under his chin and her ass nestled into his lap.

He didn't know what he would do when she woke up and found herself in bed with a yeti, but all he could do was hope that the same accepting spirit of Charles also lived in her.

Chapter 9

Stefania

She was wrapped in a shag carpet. A warm, fuzzy, heavy shag carpet that was... vibrating?

She cracked open an eyelid. The room was pitch black. She was curled on her side, warm and mostly comfortable, though her body ached and her head throbbed. Was she in the middle of another migraine episode? Stefania groaned, shifting her hips back in the bed, and the buzzing against her shoulder blades abruptly increased speed.

Her head swam from the small movement and she closed her eye again, deciding to drift back off and see if she could sleep off the migraine. She pulled a hand out from under the covers and absently rubbed at the soft furry blanket draped across her abdomen. The vibration ratcheted up another gear, turning into a deep rumble. Seriously, was there a pack of purring cats nearby? Had she accidentally left a vibrator on underneath the sheets?

A deep, masculine voice suddenly sounded from close behind her. *Very* close behind her.

"Are you all right?"

She startled fully awake, but the heavy blanket around her waist was wrapped tight and didn't let her go far. Nothing was visible in the darkness of the room, and she didn't know *that* voice- she would've remembered it. She tried to struggle against confines of the blanket, her sore body protesting every movement. "Where am I? Who are *you*?"

The deep voice spoke slow and soothing, like he was trying to placate a frightened animal. She supposed she *was* a frightened animal. "Please stay calm- it is all right. I do not want you to further injure yourself. I am sorry I scared you. My name is Oswald." The bass rumble of his voice echoed through her bones and caused a slight shiver to course its way down her spine. "You fell into the river and I brought you back to my cabin to get you warm. Please try to stay still."

Stefania stiffened, the memories of the river, the bear, and the bloodcurdling roar she'd heard as she went underwater beginning to flood back in. "I...the bear... you saved me?"

The blanket around her waist tightened a bit more, and she pulled at it a bit to give some it some slack. It was warm, solid, and definitely furry. *Is this a dog draped over me?* She ran her hand gently through the fur and felt it shudder slightly. Definitely a dog. She relaxed a bit and petted it again.

"I did," Oswald replied gravely. His voice had a slight accent that she couldn't place, as well as a small speech impediment, but it flowed like warm honey over her bones. "I had to take some liberties with your clothing to get your temperature up and I apologize for that."

Stefania's cheeks heated, realizing she was bare naked under this blanket. The voice was right above her head- had he been spooning her and using his own body heat to keep her warm? *I thought that was just a silly book trope.* She felt a fluffy towel wrapped around herself- at least there was the towel and the dog between herself and the man. *Did he have to cut my clothes off of me?*

"I am so sorry," the man said again, sounding genuinely contrite. "It was the only thing I could think to do. We were too far out in the woods to get to a hospital, and you were turning blue."

Stefania searched vainly in the dark for a clock or even her phone. The house seemed to be devoid of electronic lights. Was this guy totally off the grid? "What time is it? And how did you find me? I didn't think there was anyone else around for miles."

She felt a puff of air on her hair as he released a breath above her. The guy must be over six and a half feet tall if she was cocooned like this.

"I was hunting in the area and heard your scream, and got there as fast as I could. Though it was not fast enough," she heard him mutter. "It may be around two o'clock- I do not have a watch, but you have been out for many hours. How are you feeling? You were tossed about pretty roughly in the river- you should go get checked out tomorrow morning."

"My head... I must've hit my head," she groaned and gingerly pressed a few fingers to her hair. There was definitely a giant goose egg on her skull.

The rumbling stopped. Was it... him? Was he the one causing the vibration?

"You did," he replied, and the words came out as a growl. She shivered again and his icy tone switched to one of concern. "Are you still cold?"

The warm weight against her back pressed harder into her. No doubt about it now, he was definitely lying in bed with her. She found that she didn't hate the idea of being perfectly spooned after her near-death experience, even if it was with a complete stranger.

Being tall herself, she had not ever experienced a perfectly slotted spoon cuddle before tonight. A woman could get used to this.

"No, I'm warm, thank you. And thank you for saving me... Oswald, was it?" The rumble at her back started back up. "Are you... shivering? Are you cold?" she asked.

He audibly gulped before he replied. "I am not cold, but I am shaking. I am sorry- I cannot seem to control it lately."

He sure apologizes a lot, she thought to herself. *Does he have a condition that makes him shake? How did he carry me here?* She was formulating a response when a thought occurred to her and she exclaimed, "Oh, *you* are Oswald! You must've known my great-uncle, Charles! He has an envelope for you in the cabin."

Her mafia romance plot regarding the mysterious Oswald would need to be modified but she could still work with this. Perhaps a grumpy/sunshine trope with a hunter from the deep woods of Alaska. Rescuing a damsel in distress? Cuddling for warmth? The story practically wrote itself.

"Charles was your great-uncle?"

She nodded, wincing in pain at the slight movement. It was dark anyways, why was she nodding? She mentally cringed at her awkwardness. "He was. I didn't even know I had a great-uncle until he died, though. I take it you knew him?"

She felt Oswald take another deep inhale behind her before he answered. The man's chest must be huge. "He was my dearest friend for many years- the best person I knew. He gave me this little hunting cabin some years ago. I didn't know he had a niece, either- he never mentioned it when he was preparing for..." Oswald hesitated, then continued. "...preparing for his death."

Stefania once again felt a pang of sadness at the missed opportunity of knowing a family member. So many people around here sung his praises, and yet she couldn't figure out why there had been no funeral or no obituary- not even a headstone or even ashes to spread. But perhaps Oswald knew the secret, knew why Charles was so distant with the world.

Her head hurt too much to want to talk about it now.

She wanted to snuggle back against him, to shut her eyes and fall back asleep in this warm cocoon, but she needed to get clothed and get home. She was exhausted and sore, but even though she was not getting creeper vibes from this man, she was still alone and practically naked in his bed in the middle of the night. No one knew where she was, and she needed the safety of her own home.

"Thank you for saving me, but I should get back to the cabin. If I didn't lose or break my phone, the map app should be able to point me in the right direction, and I'm sure you would like your sleep."

The furry dog on her abdomen shifted, and she petted it again. *This dog is so soft*, she noted. "I do not have a car or a snowmobile, but I can carry you to the cabin if you really want to go- it is about a fifteen-minute walk through the woods if I take it slow."

"I can't ask you to carry me- I should be able to walk just fine." Her head pounded in protest even as she said the words.

A small grunt came from Oswald's direction. "You have hit your head- it is safer if I carry you. You are quite light and it is no trouble at all."

She barely suppressed her snort. She was almost six feet tall and curvy- not exactly a featherweight. Maybe this guy moonlighted as a bodybuilder? It would explain how he carried her to his cabin, although she didn't know where it was in reference to the river; he could've carried her ten yards for all she knew. But he was probably right about her walking alone in the cold and dark with a head wound, especially if her clothes were still wet. And if she had a concussion? Not smart. But she didn't feel totally comfortable staying here with this stranger, no matter warm she was or how velvety his deep voice sounded.

She sighed in resignation. "If you're really okay with it- I'd like to go back to the cabin."

"Very well," replied Oswald. She could feel him hesitate again behind her. "We can wrap you in the blanket to keep you warm. I have to warn you- I am not quite what you are expecting, and I do not want you to be scared."

"...Okay...?" Was she suddenly in *The Phantom of the Opera*?

The dog slid slowly off of her stomach and the man shifted away from her back, and she immediately missed their combined warmth and weight. Either she was still suffering from the fall into the river or the house they were in didn't have much insulation. Alaskan winters were no joke.

She heard him take a deep breath and exhale slowly. "I am not like other men you might have seen. I am... different." He paused. "A little furrier."

Stefania's throat constricted, a frisson of worry zinging up her neck. He sounded so nervous. How bad could it be? "You could look like Grizzly Adams and I wouldn't care, you saved my life and I am eternally grateful. Is there a light in here?"

"There is a small lamp on the table next to you, with a switch on the base."

Stefania felt for the switch and clicked on the bedside lamp, illuminating the small room.

The first thing she noticed was a carved figurine next to the lamp. An eagle? One of Charles', she surmised.

The next thing she noticed was there was no dog in the bed.

But there *was* fur. Lots and lots of white fur.

A *massive* mound of white fur. That had arms. And legs. And claws. And a face with fangs.

And... it spoke?

"Stefania?"

She blinked. She must've *really* hit her head. She was seeing the Abominable Snowman. Served her right for watching *Rudolph the Red-Nosed Reindeer* last week- her subconscious was telling her it was too early for holiday movies.

"Bumble?"

"No. I am Oswald."

She blinked again. The voice from the Abominable Snowman matched the velvet bass tone of the man that had saved her life. "You are... Oswald?"

It held itself perfectly still, save a faint rumbling she could hear in its chest. This was a dream. She was still asleep. Or had she fallen in the river and actually drowned? Was she dead?

It spoke again.

"I am. Please do not be afraid- I will not hurt you."

She heaved herself into a sitting position and clutched the soft towel around her body. Everything ached. Surely if she was dead she wouldn't still hurt like this. A dream, then. "What... what are you?"

The creature slowly, so slowly raised one massive arm and held a hand out to her, palm up. It was a massive hand, covered in light bluish-gray hair and tipped with wicked-looking black claws on each finger and thumb. "I am a yeti."

Stefania reached out and tentatively touched the large paw, stroking a finger down the upturned palm. She didn't miss the slight shudder that worked its way through the creature's body. "A yeti? I thought they were a myth."

"There are not very many of us. We normally do not allow ourselves to be seen by humans."

She raised her eyes to his face (she assumed he was a male, given the deep voice and the name Oswald), taking it in. His features were covered in the same blue-grey fur as his hands, with a soft white beard rounding out the bottom half and partially covering a wide mouth. Bright white fangs poked down over each side of the bottom lip. At the top of his head, two spiky black horns emerged out of the white fur, each about three or four inches tall.

His eyes, though- under a pair of bushy white eyebrows sat bright blue eyes the color of glacier water, and it felt as though those eyes were staring down into her very soul. She clutched his hand reflexively and stared back at him, at a loss for words.

Their staring contest stretched on. Stefania was beginning to think that maybe she wasn't dreaming. Was this actually real? Was she looking at an actual, real life mythical creature? A mythical creature that was *purring*?

Oswald opened that wide mouth and she got a glimpse of

more sharp white teeth as he said, "Stefania? Are you... are you okay?"

Stefania couldn't help her snort, which turned into a giggle. *I must be going insane.* She finally realized she was still holding onto his paw and released it, still giggling. "You are a yeti. A real, live yeti. And... you knew my great-uncle? My great-uncle knew about you?"

She took a moment to pinch herself in the arm. Nope, she was definitely awake. She was awake, sore, and chatting with a yeti.

Ah, Alaska.

Oswald slowly withdrew his hand back to his side and eased into a sitting position next to her. She took the opportunity to look over the rest of him- he was enormous, and she could tell that underneath the soft white fur were muscles upon muscles upon muscles. Now she didn't wonder how he'd carried her- he was built like a linebacker. *No,* she corrected herself- *linebackers would be lucky to be built like* him.

She took a second to congratulate herself on how well she was compartmentalizing this entire encounter. She might crumble into a quivering heap once reality set in, but for now she was cool, calm, and collected.

"I did know Charles," he rumbled. She didn't think she'd ever get tired of hearing that voice. "He saved my life, found me when I was caught in a bear trap. He freed me and kept me safe while I healed."

She nodded, her brain still processing the day's events. Bear. Yeti. River. Cabin. The cabin- she needed to get back to the cabin. She could freak out about this later.

"I should really get back. Do you think my clothes are dry?"

Oswald looked away- bashfully, she thought. "I am afraid I was in a rush to get them off of you and get you warm- I had to cut them off of you."

Moving very slowly (as to not spook her, she supposed), he got off the bed and went into another room. Seeing him rise to his full height took her breath away- he had to be over seven feet tall. Her gaze followed the massive creature as he approached her with an armful of strips of cloth. She recognized the remains of her bra and groaned inwardly- that was one of her favorite bras and they weren't cheap. Her jacket and socks were the only items that weren't in ribbons. Nothing else appeared to be salvageable.

Oswald looked down at the floor. "I am very sorry, Stefania. You can keep that towel around you and I will keep you as warm as possible on the walk back."

She bit her lip and stared up at the yeti. "You saved my life, Oswald." His eyes snapped up to hers and his chest rumbled. She smiled at him and the rumbling increased. "I'm willing to overlook the damage to my clothes if it means I'm alive."

Oswald's blue eyes bored into hers with such intensity that she had to look away after a moment and busied herself with checking the condition of her phone, which had been in her thankfully zipped jacket pocket. The case was cracked, but the phone itself still worked. She sent up a prayer of thanks to the universe.

Once her socks and jacket were on and she was firmly wrapped in the towel, Stefania stood up- only to immediately sit back down on the mattress. Oswald reached out a steadying hand.

"I'm okay, just a head rush," she told him. "Can I use your bathroom for a minute?"

He took her elbow gently and showed her to the bathroom. She noticed he was incredibly mindful of not nicking her with his sharp claws. When she was done with the toilet, she stood to wash her hands and got a glimpse of herself in the mirror over the sink. Holy moly- she looked terrible.

Her face was pale and drawn tight with dark circles under her eyes, and hair was a mess. She grimaced at her reflection and gingerly touched her scalp where she hit her head. A clean brush sat next to the sink, and she decided to try and untangle a bit of the mess and braid it before they trekked back through the cold and it froze like this.

Brushing her hair proved to be a problem, though, as her shoulder and ribcage ached too badly to properly raise her arms over her head. She was in the middle of grimacing at herself when a knock sounded on the door.

She triple-checked the tightness of the towel wrapped around her. "You can come in," she called.

The door opened and Oswald stuck his head in. His gaze took in the brush in her hand and the expression of pain on her face. "Would you like for me to do that?"

She slumped against the sink and wordlessly handed the brush to him. This was her life. A yeti was going to brush her hair.

Oswald came up behind her and began to gently untangle the knots at the bottom of her hair, carefully working his way up and avoiding her head wound. She didn't want to admit to herself that his ministrations felt wonderful and soothing. Tingles worked their way down her spine as he tenderly sifted the brush and his claws through her hair.

She watched him in the mirror as he worked, full concentration on his task. He wasn't so scary like this. Sure, he towered over her and took up most of the room with his broad muscular stature, but he seemed to be kind and gentle. *Sort of like the Beast from Beauty and the Beast.*

"I put some ointment on your scratch up here," he said, pointing to her scalp with the claw of one finger. "You should be fine for now, but in the morning you should put more on it."

"Thank you again for saving me," she said softly. "I thought for sure that I was going to die."

He glanced at her in the mirror, his piercing blue eyes once again looking directly into her soul.

"I will protect you, no matter what."

The earnestness in that deep voice sent another frisson of pleasure down her spine.

Chapter 10

Oswald

Oswald could hardly believe it. Here he was, trudging through the forest with his mate in his arms. He never would have pictured this moment in a thousand years. She was soft and warm in the cradle of his embrace, and once again it took most of his concentration to force his body to obey his commands and keep all of his blood from running straight to his cock. He had behaved while she was asleep, his concern for her wellbeing overriding the demands of his body telling him to *claim, claim, claim...* but now that she was awake- and better yet, seemingly not scared of him- all blood threatened to course southward to his groin.

If it wasn't so cold out for her fragile human body, he'd take the long way through the forest and extend the pleasure of holding her so close to him. But instead, he carefully wound his way through the trees on a direct path to the cabin, taking great pains to not bounce her around.

His chest had settled into a constant, quiet rumble of contentment. Oswald didn't remember ever hearing either of his parents make a noise like the one he was currently making- a slow, rolling purr. What did it mean? Did it only occur during the courtship, before a pair was properly mated? Did it only occur if you were bursting with joy? Had his parents never been this happy?

She lifted her head from where it was tucked against his chest, her braid of auburn hair coiling around her shoulder. He couldn't believe she'd let him brush her hair *and* braid it into a simple plait. His heart had almost beat itself right out of his chest when his claws were in her strands, and he had to remind himself that she didn't know the significance of what he was doing for her.

Yeti-folk were very fastidious creatures, and brushing the fur of your mate was one of the most loving and sentimental acts a yeti could perform.

"You have a lot of carvings in your house," Stefania observed. Her voice was low and soft, and he'd go to the ends of the earth just to hear her say his name again. "Did Charles make all of them for you?"

Oswald took a deep breath, expanding his chest as he tried to think quickly. He didn't like the idea of lying to her, but he wasn't ready for her to find out that he was the one who made the figurines (he'd spotted *The Hug* through the dining room window one day) or that he'd been the one to leave the wooden box at her door. So much had happened already today, more than he could've ever dreamed, and he wasn't sure how she would react to knowing he was the artist behind them.

Then again, she'd taken the fact that she'd been rescued by a yeti with a surprising amount of calm.

"He did not carve them for me, no." There- not necessarily a lie. Charles hadn't carved them at all.

"Oh," Stefania murmured, laying her head back on his chest.

The silence stretched, and Oswald frantically searched through his thoughts for something to say. Finally, he settled on asking about Charles. "You mentioned that you did not know that Charles existed... your family never mentioned him?"

She blew out a breath, the exhalation causing some of the fur on his chest to ruffle and sending a tremor of pleasure through his body. He concentrated yet again on not unsheathing his cock. Every movement of her body, every whiff of her delicious scent, every little thing about her made the primal part of his brain roar in triumph and *need*.

He was glad that he had a firmer control on himself than that first night he'd seen her and gone berserk with lust. He could be calmer, even if tightly leashed.

"No, they didn't. But my mom died years ago and my father was never in the picture. No grandparents to speak of either- on my mom's side, they passed away in a house fire when she was away at boarding school. Everything in the house was lost- no photo albums or records were ever recovered."

She blew out another sigh, and Oswald barely contained his shudder. After a moment, she continued on. "I don't understand why Charles never contacted me- why wait until after he's gone?"

Oswald's heart constricted at how small her voice sounded. She was hurt, he realized- deeply hurt over the perceived rejection of a family member when she believed herself alone in this world.

"I do not know- he did not tell me he had a great-niece, either. He did not speak much of his family or how he had ended up in Alaska."

Stefania raised her head to look at him with those beautiful green eyes. He kept his gaze firmly on the ground, trying to focus on picking his way through the forest as safely as possible. The moon shone off the snow and illuminated the forest brightly enough that Oswald could easily see where he was going. Even if he didn't already know this route like the back of his paw, he still didn't want to trip and fall while he was carrying her.

Her next question was soft and curious, no hint of fear or disgust lacing the words. "How did *you* end up in Alaska?"

Oswald glanced down at her for a split second, taking in the sight in his arms. Even bundled up in the odd combination of a towel, jacket, and socks with his blanket wrapped around her for extra warmth, she was stunning. The auburn hair, green eyes, full lips, and soft curves that encased strong muscles- just perfect.

Perfect for him.

He gave her a small smile and noted how her glance darted to his fangs and back to his eyes. "How much do you want to know?"

"Everything," she replied with a smile of her own.

"I am afraid I cannot give you a good detailed history of the yeti clans, as I was usually not paying attention when my parents were lecturing me. They- my mother and father, I mean- migrated from the Himalayas before I was born. They passed away long ago, falling into a crevasse on Denali. I liked the area and stayed here until I met Charles, who rescued me from a bear trap. As far as I know, there are no other yeti-folk in the area."

"I'm so sorry about your parents," Stefania told him with sincerity in her eyes.

"I am sorry to hear about your mother as well, Stefania."

It wasn't the first time he'd said her name tonight, but this time, her eyes narrowed slightly. "I don't think I ever told you my name."

Icy panic shot through his veins. She definitely hadn't told him her name, but he couldn't reveal that he'd overheard it while he was watching and waiting for his courtship gift to be accepted- he'd come away looking like a perverted, crazy monster. Which, he amended, he supposed he was. But he would prefer not to look like it on the first night they officially met.

He inwardly groaned and decided he could only omit so much information in one night. Time for another partial truth. "I heard Henry say it yesterday morning while he was on your front porch. I was in the woods."

She snorted and immediately winced at the pain it caused. "He did practically scream it." She paused, then added, "You were in the woods? Are... are you often in the woods around the cabin?"

His mind immediately jumped to observing her in the shower, and he forced down the visceral reaction to the memory. "The cabin is on my hunting loop. I pass it from time to time." Not a lie- the whole forest was his hunting grounds, and if "time to time" really meant *every day*, it still was true.

Stefania nodded against his chest and gazed at the path ahead, going quiet.

All he could think about as he trudged closer to the cabin was how much he wanted those green eyes back on him.

Oswald nudged open the back door of the cabin and squeezed through the door frame. Logically, he knew that it would've been slightly easier to set Stefania on her feet and let her enter first, but he didn't want to relinquish his hold just yet.

She motioned in the direction of the bedroom, seemingly content to stay in his arms. "I think I'd like to get some more sleep."

Oswald nodded and moved through the kitchen, noting all the improvements Stefania had made in the few short weeks that she'd been here. "The house looks great. I like what you have done to it."

Stefania peered up at him again. "Have you been in here often?" .

He nodded again as they passed through the great room. Maybe he should build her a fire in the wood stove so the house would be warmer. "After my accident, Charles brought me here for my recovery. I stayed in a bed in the guest room for many weeks. He taught me your language, gave me things to keep my mind occupied."

"He taught you English?"

"He did," Oswald confirmed. "Very slowly. The shape of

my fangs makes pronouncing words difficult, as I am sure you noticed."

"English is a hard language to learn- so many nuances. I think you sound fantastic." She patted him absently as she said it, and he shuddered involuntarily as his chest rumbled with pleasure. She glanced at his chest. "I know you mentioned you can't control the shaking. Are you... purring? Do yetis purr?"

He gently set her down on her feet. "I... I do not know. I cannot recall ever hearing my parents make this sort of noise." His skin was hot with embarrassment underneath his fur, and he couldn't look her in the eyes. He began fussing with the bed covers, turning them back so she could crawl in between the sheets.

Stefania ducked into the closet and came out a few minutes later, clad in a pair of flannel pajamas. Beelining for the bed, she curled her body underneath the blankets and leaned back on her pillow, releasing a long sigh as she settled. "I think it's cute."

Cute?

Him?

He didn't have a response to that.

She sighed again and closed her eyes. "I'm going to sleep now, Oswald. Thank you for saving my life tonight."

He couldn't help it. He knew he shouldn't- it would freak her out, she would scream and throw him out- but the desire to claim her in some fashion thrummed through his veins. He leaned down and brushed his lips against her temple, gently as to not cause any more pain. He pulled away and held his breath, but she merely tucked her head further into the pillow and gave a small, sleepy smile.

He made sure she was covered with plenty of blankets and turned off the bedroom lights, shutting the door behind him as he stepped out of the room. His mind whirled with the events of the evening. He'd met his mate- saved her, held her, kissed her forehead. And she hadn't been scared of him.

She hadn't been scared of him.

She had accepted the fact that he was a yeti. Sure, she hit her head and maybe she thought she was still dreaming and might snap out of it, but she had seen him, accepted him, and talked to him. Asked questions about him and shared a little of her past as well.

Was it possible that his courtship plans might *actually* come to fruition? Could a human as perfect as herself possibly consider him as a potential mate?

A small kernel of hope bloomed to life within him as he built a fire for his mate.

Chapter 11

Stefania

Stefania woke slowly, the aches and pains of her body reminding her of the ordeal she had been through yesterday. She stretched slowly, taking stock of the condition of her battered body. Achy head, tender ribs, sore shoulder. But all things considered, she was happy to be alive and mostly functional, and most of all happy to not be bear food.

And she had met Oswald.

Oswald, a *yeti*.

Oswald, a yeti with a beautifully deep voice who had rescued her and taken such great pains to keep her safe and warm.

Oswald, a yeti who had carried her home in his strong arms without any effort or complaint in the middle of the night. She had felt safe, secure, and... cherished?

She pondered that thought as she got out of bed and began her morning routine, showering and swapping out her flannel pajamas for black leggings and a cropped t-shirt. This couldn't be a normal feeling, but what was normal anymore? All sense of normalcy had flown out the window the second she learned that yetis (yeti-folk, he'd called them) existed and one had saved her life. Not only that, but he had treated her with such gentleness and care, even going as far as to brush and braid her hair.

Stefania briefly imagined the feeling of black claws gently raking through her scalp when her wounds healed. It would probably feel amazing, like one of those metal scalp massagers she loved so much. Shivery tingles worked their way down her arms just from thinking about the glorious sensation.

Although… would she even see him again before she left, or would he remain hidden for the remainder of her time in Alaska? She supposed she could go searching for his little cabin, although she didn't even know which direction to look. She hadn't exactly been the most coherent during their trek through the forest.

A thought struck her, making her pause over the coffee maker. A yeti- a sweet, sensitive, gentle giant of a yeti- lived on this land. What would happen to him when she sold everything? What would he do if the new owner decided to tear down his cabin? Where would he go?

Would he be safe?

She was leaving in about a month, if her renovation timeline worked out as planned. She'd already met with Kim, the real estate agent that Ana had recommended. Kim would handle the photos and listing of the house once renovations were complete, and per Kim's recommendation, the house would be listed on New Year's Day instead of Christmas. She had time to tell Oswald of her plans so he could prepare. He'd survived on his own before, so surely he'd be able to find somewhere else to live if the circumstances called for it.

Right?

Stefania poured herself a cup of coffee and checked the weather forecast on her phone. A snow storm was expected to come through tomorrow evening, and she hoped that the appliance installation would be finished before the storm hit.

After she found a doctor to check her over, she'd visit the Winterhaven Market today and grab some extra supplies and fuel for the generator.

Another thought crossed her mind. *Will Oswald be okay during the storm?*

She was raising her coffee cup to her lips, contemplating the thermal capacity of that soft, luscious yeti fur when she heard a thump on the front porch. She cracked open the front door and peered outside.

The last thing she expected to see was Oswald, muscular arms stretched over his massive frame, concentrating heavily on fiddling with something on the porch roof. Had he even gone home?

He is freaking enormous. Look at those biceps! No wonder he had no problem carrying me.

She wasn't dressed for an Alaskan November morning, so she opened the door just wide enough to stick her head out. "Oswald?"

He visibly twitched and stared at her, clearly surprised. His face relaxed into a soft smile after a few moments and he replied, "Stefania, good morning! How are you feeling?"

She shrugged, forgetting he couldn't see the rest of her through the door. Not the best thing to do, as her shoulder twinged from the movement. "I'm achy, but alive."

His features seemed to momentarily darken with anger, but she blinked and the expression was gone. "Glad to hear it," he rumbled in that deep voice. He finished whatever he was doing with the roof and relaxed those big arms by his sides, his gaze settling on her once again. "Do you feel well enough to go to town to see a doctor?"

"I'll be fine to drive once the coffee kicks in."

Those glacier-blue eyes lasered into her own, and she couldn't help but feel struck by the intensity of his gaze. After a moment he nodded, but said nothing else. In the silence, she could hear the reverberation coming from his chest, faint but steady.

This was awkward.

What am I supposed to do with a yeti?

Her manners kicked in. "I'll make some breakfast before going to the clinic. Would you like to come in? I'll make you something as well, if you're hungry."

The reverberation stuttered, then continued a little louder. She found it endearing.

He nodded again and slowly approached her as she opened the door wider for him. Pausing directly in front of her, he lifted a huge hand to her face and gently gripped her chin in his claws. Startled, she kept still as his eyes roved over her features, taking stock of her injuries. Seemingly satisfied with what he saw, he softly ran a claw over her jawline and released her.

"I would like that very much, thank you."

A delicious shiver worked its way down Stefania's spine at his touch, and she felt her cheeks growing hot as those blue eyes held her gaze for a few moments. She moved to the side as he entered, closing the door behind him and bustling into the kitchen in an attempt to hide her nerves. It wasn't fear she was feeling... it was something else, an emotion she couldn't name and didn't want to analyze too closely at the moment.

"Bacon, eggs, French toast? Pancakes? Any preference?" She paused at the refrigerator and turned to look at him. "How much do you usually eat? Are you even hungry? Can you even eat human food?"

Chuckling, Oswald made his way to the tall bar-height island that separated the kitchen and dining room, settling on one of the sturdy stools so easily it looked like he'd done it a thousand times. He probably had, she realized. Those stools had initially seemed so thick and cumbersome to her, but now she wondered if they had been procured or built specifically with Oswald in mind. This massive white creature was perfectly at home in this kitchen, his heavy arms resting on the top of the island as he casually leaned over it.

"Charles introduced me to human food, and I can assure you, I like it all. Normally yeti-folk subsist on meat- fresh meat," he supplied, glancing at her as if he expected her to be repulsed. "We tend to eat a lot in the warmer seasons to prepare for the colder weather when the…" -he paused again- "…meat… is not as available."

"So how much should I make you?"

The corners of his lips tipped up, revealing a little bit more of his fangs. They were so white and clean- did he brush them like humans did? What about flossing? "You can make me a regular human-sized portion. I would not want to eat you out of house and home."

Stefania tried not to blush at the words *eat you out* while she surreptitiously snuck another glance at his fangs. *Of course he didn't mean it like that!* She scolded herself silently as she switched on the old stovetop. *First it's mafia romances, now you're imagining yourself in a monster romance novel.*

Breakfast turned out to be a very pleasant affair. Despite his insistence at only needing a human-sized portion, she cooked a generous spread of her favorite breakfast foods and he seemed to take great pleasure in sampling it all. His favorite was the French toast, tucking into the stack with gusto when Stefania set the plate in front of him.

At first, she wasn't sure if he could even grip a utensil with those big claws of his, but Oswald had risen and plucked a huge wooden spork out of a kitchen drawer, demonstrating that the handle had been carved specifically for him. He'd then proceeded to devour everything she gave him with enthusiasm, looking slightly sheepish once he was finished.

She thought it was adorable. She loved that he enjoyed her cooking, and even though he worked his way through the food at an alarming rate, his manners were still impeccable and he even managed to chew with his mouth closed despite the impediment of fangs. She wondered if he was doing that on her account or if he usually took such care with eating.

The conversation flowed easily between them, with Oswald asking questions about herself and her work as a graphic designer, particularly focusing on her favorite style inspirations. She discovered that he loved art and shyly offered to show him some of her latest pieces of work after breakfast.

His instantaneous enthusiastic agreement made her giggle. She mentally rolled her eyes at herself at being reduced to a blushing, giggling teenager, but she couldn't bring herself to care too much. After working so hard for weeks on end, she was relaxed and enjoying herself (and his company) immensely.

Throughout breakfast his gaze was often on the statue of *The Hug*, and she found herself explaining how she had been drawn to that statue, to that desire to make a deep connection with another. Oswald had quietly murmured his agreement, piercing her yet again with an icy blue stare.

Was he as lonely out here as she was? What would happen when she left and he was alone again- and potentially homeless as well? Would he make himself known to any other humans if the loneliness got too much to bear? What if they weren't as accepting as she was?

Despite spending the morning talking to him, she found that she couldn't yet voice the words about her plans to sell the house and surrounding lands. She knew the longer she waited, the worse it would be, and yet- she couldn't bring herself to tell him. He deserved to know that he would lose his home soon, but she wanted to enjoy his company for just a bit longer. He was attentive, kind, intelligent, and so easy to talk to that she pushed the thoughts to the back of her mind.

She knew it was wrong, but it would be a problem for future Stefania, not present-day Stefania.

Early Tuesday morning, the snow fell.

And fell.

And fell.

A little over two feet of snow had fallen in a matter of hours, covering the already snowy landscape in fresh powder. Stefania had prepared for the blizzard with the help of Ana, Bridget, and Henry, who had dropped by the cabin Monday morning to make sure Charles' old snowblower was still functional in case she needed it. He had handed her another small package he'd found on her front porch, wrapped in that same faded paper- this time, it was a beautiful carving of two otters holding hands as though they were drifting in the sea. She briefly recalled telling Oswald that otters were one of her favorite animals, and she wondered if the yeti had found it in his stash of carvings... but did that mean that the little wooden keepsake box was also from Oswald?

But that couldn't be the case, as they hadn't even met when the box had been left on her front porch. Or perhaps Henry was playing some elaborate prank on her and the carvings were from him. She ordered one of those new doorbell cameras with a motion detector, just in case the presents continued.

After being cleared by a doctor yesterday, she stopped by the Winterhaven Market to be fussed over then immediately reamed up one side and down the other for hiking on her own so close to dusk. Stefania told Ana only that she'd slipped and fell in the river, leaving out the fact that she'd been trying to escape a bear (and the subsequent rescue-by-yeti). Dropping into Beans, Beans to see Bridget and grab another veggie wrap was much the same- concern over her well-being, followed by a scolding. Stefania endured it all, secretly pleased that there were friends in this little town that cared enough about her to tell her that she'd been an idiot.

She had returned home that evening to see all of the Christmas lights from Ana's stash strung up along the front of the cabin, illuminating the house in a soft glow. The home had been transformed into a lone beacon of beautiful color in the monochromatic Alaskan forest. She'd stopped and stared at the picturesque scene, admiring the loveliness of the rustic cabin and the surrounding land. Alaska was worming its way into her heart, harsh winters and all.

She realized Oswald must've been putting up the lights that morning, and the warm affection she felt towards the yeti expanded a little more in her chest. He'd been gone when she returned from town and she had not seen him since. And as silly as it was- even though she hadn't known him but for less than a day- she found herself missing his calm, solid presence.

She had plenty of food, water, and fuel for her generator, and she was fully prepared to hunker down for a while and enjoy the quiet of the snow. It a slow week at work since most of her team was out for the Thanksgiving holiday, and she planned on using some of the downtime to decompress with art and reading- and perhaps enjoy all the sparkling new kitchen appliances that had been installed throughout the day. Maybe she'd draw Oswald if the mood struck.

And so, Stefania spent Monday evening and much of Tuesday morning curled up on the couch with a blanket and an alien romance book, a pleasant fire crackling away merrily in the wood stove. By Tuesday afternoon, she was contemplating braving the bracing bitterness of the still-falling snow to retrieve more wood when she heard a knock at the door. She opened it to find a giant on the front porch, a large axe propped on his boulder-like shoulder.

Stefania *screamed* and flailed her arms, frantically backing away from the open door. Oswald, realizing that maybe he looked a bit like an axe murderer, immediately dropped the axe on the porch and held up his big hands. "Stefania, wait! It is me, Oswald! I came to see if you wanted any wood chopped!"

Stefania held a hand to her heart and another to her forehead as she took in a few deep, shuddering breaths. "You scared the crap out of me, Oswald!"

Oswald took a tentative step closer to the open door. "I am so sorry, I did not mean to frighten you. It is the last thing I want to do. Are you well?"

No, you just gave me a heart attack!

She gave him a tremulous smile as she gathered herself together and waved him inside. "Come in, please. I'm fine- just didn't expect anyone today, especially a giant with an axe. Maybe a warning next time?"

He started to reach out to touch her arm and seemed to catch himself, lowering his hand back to his side. She glanced briefly at the hand, at those sharp black claws that she had fantasized about. It flexed open for a second and her eyes snapped back up to his face.

"I am sorry," he told her again, his deep voice soft and honest, his eyes seeming to drink in the details of her as he looked her over. "How are you feeling?"

She shuffled back to the big worn leather couch that had been her nest for the past 24 hours and waved at him to sit down. "Sore, but otherwise feeling better. The doctor said it was a miracle I didn't break anything during the river incident." She grimaced. "Have I thanked you enough for saving my life?"

Oswald gave her a small smile as he joined her on the couch, resting in the corner of the sectional with a long, muscular arm draped along the back. His big body looked comfortable in that spot and she wondered if he had sat in that same position with Charles. "You can thank me as much as you feel you need to, though it is unnecessary. To know that you are safe and well is thanks enough."

Stefania didn't quite know what to say to that, and Oswald continued after a moment. "I came to see if you needed any more wood for your fire- I know Charles had some large logs set aside to dry out but they have not been split yet. I can chop them for you if you like."

A sense of gratefulness bloomed in her chest. This yeti was so thoughtful that he trekked through a blizzard to see if she needed more firewood. Sure, he'd scared the shit out of her (and she was slightly embarrassed by *that* reaction) but that hadn't been his intention. Perhaps unconsciously, she angled her body towards him as she tucked her legs beneath her. "I'd love more wood."

Why did I put it like that?

She blushed furiously and looked down at her hands, hoping that he wouldn't understand the human colloquialism and how it sounded like she was saying she wanted his cock. But there was no change in his expression or in the ever-present quiet purr of his chest, nothing to indicate that he took her statement as any more than her wanting chopped up firewood.

Definitely not his cock. She definitely, definitely didn't want his cock.

Although now that she thought about it… where *was* it? Though he was covered in thick white fur, surely she would've seen something by now or at least felt something when his large body had been pressed against hers for warmth on that first fateful night. Did he not have one?

Oh no. No, no, no. Now she was thinking too much about his cock.

Oswald thankfully had no idea her train of thought had been so epically derailed. The hand draped so casually across the back of the couch stretched towards her, as if he could not help himself. "I will bring more wood in here for you."

Stefania's face flamed again as she mentally berated herself. *You are in your late thirties, for crying out loud! You are not a twelve-year-old boy. Get your mind out of the gutter.* "Thanks, Oswald. I really appreciate it. Can I get you anything to eat?"

The black claws that had been inching closer to her slowly reached out and gently snagged a lock of red hair that had fallen out of the braid. Her heart thumped wildly within her chest and she sat perfectly still as he wound the strand around his thick, bluish-gray fingers. Was he… was he leaning in closer?

Her breath caught in her throat when one of his claws trailed across her neck, sending goosebumps across her entire body.

Oswald seemed to catch himself and released the strand of hair, his body relaxing back against the couch. He grinned at her, showing the full length of his white fangs. "I will never turn down a chance to eat. Especially if it means I get to eat what *you* prepare."

Why did her brain immediately interpret that as flirting? What was *happening* to her? Maybe the alien romance she'd been reading was not a good idea. It was giving her... *thoughts* about this yeti in front of her.

Stefania spent the afternoon watching Oswald chop wood from the warmth and safety of the kitchen, staring out the window as the enormous yeti split the giant logs into manageable chunks of firewood. Again and again, he swung that axe like a well-oiled machine, his back and shoulder muscles bunching and rippling with each precise strike.

The immense display of strength and power was so distracting that it had taken her twice as long to make dinner. He worked out there for hours, never stopping or slowing down. The sheer stamina he possessed was impressive. Not once had he complained- indeed, he seemed downright cheerful after all of his hard work, happily accepting the yeti-sized bowl of beef stew she offered him at the end of the day.

She was amazed and so grateful to him that she invited him to have Thanksgiving dinner with her in a couple of days, and he lit up with so much joy from the invitation that she thought that perhaps deep down, he really was just as starved for affection as she was.

In the evening, Stefania stepped into the large shower stall and cranked up the water temperature to near-scalding, thankful that her power had remained on throughout the blizzard and hopeful that it would continue to stay on as the temperature plummeted. Oswald had left about twenty minutes ago after restocking the pile of wood near her stove. It was still snowing, and she worried that maybe she should've asked him to stay in the guest room instead of sending him back out into the bitter cold.

She reminded herself that he was a yeti, and therefore was

perfectly suited to this kind of weather. He clearly thrived in it, if today's exhibition of muscles had been any indication.

Those muscles...

She reminisced over the afternoon scene in her backyard as she soaped up her body. Oswald was so strong. So capable. So masculine. Nothing at all like Doug the Drag. No, Oswald was the kind of male that would worship the ground you walked on while also completely and totally ravaging you every night. She could just tell- he'd be a beast in the bedroom, no pun intended.

She shook her head. What was she thinking? Was she seriously having these kinds of thoughts about a yeti? Even though that yeti was so very sweet. So very gentle. So very... furry. He was a *yeti*, for goodness' sake. She groaned and shook her head again, trying to dispel the thoughts.

Stefania realized she'd been languidly soaping her breasts while her thoughts had strayed, a familiar ache beginning to settle in her core.

She sighed and decided to give herself over to the fantasy. There was no harm in fantasizing about a sweet, muscular guy, was there? Even if he was almost seven feet tall, covered in soft white fur, and had fangs that could probably rip her throat out.

She cupped her breasts, imagining how it would feel if it were his hand, his claws, his mouth. He'd be in such awe of her that he'd knead and massage them for a while, worshiping her, enjoying the feel of her. Then he'd grow bolder and pinch her nipples between his claws and pull on them to get that exquisite mix of torturous pleasure and pain sometimes she enjoyed. Perhaps he'd scrape his fangs over the sensitive tips-

She gasped and dragged a hand down her body to her center, sliding her fingers through the slickness and swirling back up over the swollen bud of her clit. She was already on edge, so close, so sensitive, just a little more pressure, just a little faster...

Out of nowhere, another fantasy popped up in in her mind- one she hadn't really entertained with any other males before.

She imagined bending him to her will, having him on his knees in front of her, those piercing blue eyes staring up at her as he devoured her. He was so big, so strong, and it wouldn't take any effort for Oswald to utterly dominate her- but she *knew* he'd let her do whatever she wanted to with him. She'd have the power over *him*. She would plant a foot on his shoulder and hold onto his horns and put that tongue to work, licking and sucking and-

"Oh my god... fuck, fuck... oh, fuuuck, *Oswald!*"

Her orgasm exploded, and she shuddered and shook uncontrollably as waves of pure bliss pulsed throughout her body. Her cries still echoed in the shower as she collapsed against the wall, completely wrung out from the intensity of the release that had blasted through her. And hell- she was no stranger to masturbating, but she hadn't come that hard in a *long* time.

Something scraped against the bathroom window, breaking Stefania's trance.

Her head snapped up towards the source of the sound and she locked eyes with the yeti whose name had been on her lips as she came.

Oswald?

She stared blankly at him.

He turned from the window and fled.

Chapter 12

Oswald

It was a couple of days until Oswald saw Stefania again. He'd managed to sneak over to her cabin each morning to leave his courting presents at the door, taking care to cover his tracks in the snow, but he couldn't bring himself to face her. He was embarrassed that he'd been caught watching her shower through the bathroom window, and yet... he wasn't *too* mortified, as it had been worth it to hear her moan his name while she pleasured herself.

His name.

Nothing had ever sounded so sweet.

It had filled his heart with hope and his cock with blood so fast that he'd gone dizzy with lust and had blindly reached for her, scraping his claws down the window and giving himself away. He'd sprinted away in an almost exact repeat of the first night he'd seen her, except he hadn't made it to his cabin before he'd taken his cock in hand and spilled himself over the forest floor, roaring so loud he swore it echoed across the Denali peak.

Her breathy cries constantly reverberated through his head,

causing him to have to pause often to get control over himself.

He was hopelessly, happily, in her thrall.

He was in his workspace off the side of his cabin, in the middle of cleaning up some wood shavings from his latest courting gift, when he heard her voice call his name again.

Oswald paused, then took a deep breath and continued tidying up the area. He was slightly worried that he was beginning to go absolutely feral and dreaming up things that weren't actually happening. He needed to get a handle on himself.

Stefania's faint voice echoed through his head again. "Oswald!"

Wait... that sounded different from the moan that he'd replayed constantly in his imagination over the last two days.

"OSWALD!"

His ears perked up- he wasn't imagining it. She was here, in this forest, close to his cabin. He stumbled out the door, unable and unwilling to stop his body as it flung itself towards the call of his mate.

Was she in trouble?

An icy feeling crept down his spine as he ran through the forest, bellowing her name. The snow was several feet deep, how was she even out here?

"Oswald?" She was close, so close...

Oswald bounded up a hill and finally saw Stefania fighting her way through the trees, the bright red hair that escaped from under her fluffy hat a fiery beacon amidst the snow-covered landscape. She turned, her eyes going wide at the half-crazed yeti charging towards her at full speed. Her gloved hands reached out to his chest as he brought himself to a sliding stop in front of her, paws automatically going to her face to check for injuries.

"Are you hurt? What is wrong?" He continued his frantic inspection of her body, checking for blood.

He bent to run a paw down her long legs and she grabbed

his horns, instantly stopping his ministrations. Even covered in gloves, the touch of her small hands on his highly sensitive horns caused the blood to heat in his veins and he stifled a deep growl. Had it really been days since he'd seen her, felt her?

Her beautiful green eyes met his and she smiled down at him, cheeks growing a little pink as she released his horns. "I'm fine, Oswald, I promise. I was trying to see if I could find your cabin."

Oswald straightened to his full height and frowned down at her. "Alone? In this snow?"

"I'm a big girl, I can handle myself." She patted his furred arm and he relaxed a little. She was fine, she was safe, she was *here*. "My first excursion into the woods was a fluke, I swear. I hike all the time in Seattle and I'm much more prepared for the Alaskan wilderness today!" She drew out a canister of bear spray from her pocket and waved it at him. His frown deepened, but she soldiered on, her words coming out in a rush.

"I wasn't sure if you were still coming to dinner tonight, since I haven't seen you since… well, since Tuesday. I've made a ton of food and I can't possibly eat it by myself. Would you still like to come have Thanksgiving with me?"

Oswald's expression slowly turned into a smile as he considered her words, staring down at his sweet, perfect mate. Did she really think he would turn down her food? He supposed this meant she forgave him for watching her while she showered. Still, he figured he should apologize for his behavior. He took one of her hands in his, careful not to pierce through her gloves with a claw.

"Stefania, I would very much like to have dinner with you. But I must apologize for my… actions… the other night. It was an invasion of privacy and I am very sorry."

Her cheeks turned bright red as she averted her eyes and waved her free hand in the air. "It's fine, it's fine. I mean, it's *not* fine to spy on people when they shower, but I… I'm not mad at you for it. And you didn't damage the window except for a few scratches."

Oswald winced. "I am sorry for that. I can pay to replace it if you need."

Stefania looked up at him again, her forehead crinkled in confusion. "You can pay? How?" She shook her head. "Oh, the envelope of cash I gave you. Never mind, it's not necessary. Can we agree to forget it happened and just move on?"

He would never be able to forget that moment, not for the rest of his life. Even if he lived a hundred lifetimes, the memory of her crying out his name as she reached her release would be forever be happily ingrained in his brain.

Oswald risked stroking a claw down her cheek and was rewarded with a small shiver wracking her body. It didn't seem to be a fear response. She... liked that.

She liked *him*.

He fought to keep control of his body, not wanting to scare her by turning into a mindless brute. He hadn't known this side of him existed before coming across her delectable scent that very first night she'd arrived. A constant drive to *claim, claim, claim* lurked beneath the surface of his skin, threatening to turn his normally placid self into an insatiable, rutting beast.

But what if... what if she *wanted* a lover like that? Like him?

The silence stretched between them as Oswald stared down at her lovely face. The truth. He'd tell her the truth and leave it to her to decide what to do. He didn't want to make her uncomfortable, but she needed to know how he felt.

"I will do whatever makes you feel comfortable, Stefania. But I do not wish to ever forget what I saw, or what I heard." He watched as the words sank in, her eyes growing wider and wider. He gently ran the claw down the side of her neck, noting how her pulse beat wildly in her throat, matching the thrumming of his chest.

She swallowed hard as another shiver worked its way through her. He noticed it all. "Oh," she replied weakly. "Um. Okay, then."

Oswald glanced down at her feet, hidden in the snow. An idea formed in his mind and he smiled. "I will come to dinner on one condition."

Stefania followed the direction of his gaze to her boots. "What condition?"

"Let me carry you back to your cabin. The snow is very deep."

She laughed. "I've already blazed a trail, so going back will be much easier for me. I can't make you carry me twice in less than a week."

"Either you let me carry you, or I will throw you over my shoulder anyways."

She put a hand on her chest and eyed him suspiciously. "You wouldn't!"

He spread his paws wide, his smile growing more devious. "Would you like to test that theory?"

In the end, Stefania chose not to call Oswald on his bluff (which was *not* a bluff) and allowed him to carry her back to the cabin. The primal side of him was slightly disappointed that he wouldn't get the chance to chase her and throw her over his shoulder, but having her tucked in his arms was the next best thing. It was the pure selfish desire to feel her close to him again that had driven him to bargain with her, although he knew he would've come to dinner whether the condition had been agreed to or not. She merely had to crook her finger at him and he would willingly follow her into the deepest crevasse.

And if he hadn't felt that way prior to dinner, he definitely felt that way after.

This particular dinner was easily the best meal of Oswald's life. He knew Stefania was an excellent cook based on the breakfast she'd made a few days ago, and eating the vast array of all the typical American Thanksgiving foods she'd prepared proved it even further. His favorite dish so far had been her pumpkin pie, which she claimed was a recipe passed down from her mother, Lily. He'd only had one slice of the pie, but he had a plan in place to steal another slice or two later.

Conversation had once again flowed seamlessly between them during dinner. He told her more about yeti culture (conveniently leaving out the courting gift rituals), stories of his parents and their casual family hikes to summit Denali, and more about what Charles had been like (conveniently leaving out that Charles had no whittling skills). In turn, Stefania told Oswald stories about her mom, childhood, and favorite places to travel. He hung on every word she said, soaking up as much information about her as he could. Not only was his mate beautiful and an amazing cook, but she was smart, funny, and charming.

He was utterly besotted.

He helped her clean the dishes and put away leftovers (not that there were many, due to Oswald's yeti-sized appetite), and then they settled on the couch. Though it was mid-afternoon, the watery winter sun had already dipped below the horizon, making it feel much later than it was. Stefania plopped down in her normal seat with a yawn, tucking her feet under her and dragging a blanket over her lap.

He loved that she felt comfortable enough around him to relax and be herself.

Oswald sat in the spot that had been his for many years-except now, he found himself deviating from his usual cushion and inching closer to Stefania. His chest vibrations had settled into a perpetual satisfied hum over the course of the afternoon. He could tell that she was getting sleepy and thought he should see himself out so she could rest, but he didn't want to leave her just yet. Every moment spent with her was precious.

A book on the coffee table caught his eye, and he leaned forward to pick it up. The cover had a fur-clad woman standing in front of a large blue man with horns and glowing blue eyes. "What sort of a book is this?"

Stefania's green eyes grew wide when she saw the book, and

she covered her mouth with one hand. "Um... it's... a science fiction book. Blue aliens from an ice planet and that kind of thing." Her cheeks tinged with pink and he glanced back down at the book in his hand. From the expression on her face, he wondered if there was more to the plot than what she was letting on.

He flipped it open to where she had placed a bookmark, with the intention of skimming a passage. "Is it any good?"

Without warning, Stefania lunged forward and made a grab for the novel. Oswald's quick reflexes had him immediately holding the book out of her reach. Normally he would hand it over to her without delay (because who was he to deny her anything), but something darker tugged at his gut. Why didn't she want him to read it? What kind of a book was it?

Their gazes held for a beat, and a true grin began to bloom on Oswald's face as understanding dawned.

Was this a romance novel between a woman and one of these blue aliens?

He couldn't resist teasing her. With one hand, he opened the book and casually turned his head towards it, breaking their eye contact only at the last second. He wasn't the fastest reader, but a couple of choice words immediately caught his attention and his chest rumbled out a laugh.

Face flaming, Stefania clamored over his lap, frantically reaching for the book as he held it farther over his head and continued to read. His grin grew wider and wider as she doubled her efforts, never breaking stride in his perusal of the book. She'd stopped at a *very* interesting point in the chapter.

Her hands grabbed onto his horns and his whole body locked up. Tingles spread from his horns down the entire length of him, and he was completely helpless against the sensation. This seemed so much more intense then when she had grabbed them earlier. Frozen in place, his shocked gaze shifted from the book to her face.

She stared down at him, seemingly just as surprised. He

sucked in a breath as he realized the position they were in- she was now kneeling on his thighs and if he tucked his chin down just a few more inches, he'd be eye level with her breasts.

Without looking away from her face, he lowered the book to the couch cushion. Her hands remained frozen on his horns, her eyes a little wild, her chest heaving with exertion and... something else.

Heart pounding, he tested the waters and slowly brought his paws to her hips. She didn't move, and he wrapped his fingers around to cup her rear, claws gently pricking into her leggings.

Her knees suddenly slipped to the outside of his thighs, making her fully straddle him and bringing them face to face. She gasped as their centers notched up and Oswald's cock threatened to immediately unsheathe itself.

They sat like that for a long moment, neither of them breaking eye contact until Stefania's hands shifted slightly on Oswald's horns, unconsciously rubbing the sensitive bases. He couldn't stop himself from closing his eyes and groaning, his claws reflexively digging into her ass.

Stefania gasped again and he immediately relaxed his hold, shame washing over him. Did he hurt her? He was kidding himself if he ever thought there was a chance she would be interested in him. He was nothing but a beast with no self-control. His mind was just making up scenarios that would never happen.

He needed to apologize and extricate himself from this situation before he scared her away.

He reluctantly opened his eyes to find her staring back at him. She still grasped his horns- why was she still holding them? He took a breath and began to speak. "I am sor-"

Stefania rubbed the base of his horns again.

Oswald barked out a moan, his pelvis involuntarily bucking up against hers. His claws clutched at her hips again and the chest vibrations stuttered like a backfiring car. His cock was so close to unsheathing itself that he was almost in pain fighting to keep it tucked away. Could he come just from horn play? He'd never tried it before but if how he was reacting to one good squeeze was any indication, he'd blow his load in less than twenty seconds- especially with the sweet scent of his mate filling his nostrils.

As he fought for control over himself, Stefania's expression morphed from wide-eyed surprise to a knowing, sultry smirk.

Oswald gulped in a breath. "Stefania..."

She continued to smirk at him.

And then, very deliberately, she twisted her grip and stroked his horns from base to tip.

Oswald's vision went white with pleasure and he bucked against her, every muscle in his body strained against the overwhelming desire to rut, rut, rut. Stefania *knew* what she was doing to him- and willingly continued to tease him, torture him, and he would gladly submit to her every whim if she just kept touching him like that. Those hands of hers were magic.

He could feel her begin to squeeze his horns again, and he gasped out her name again in warning. Sensing that he was close to the edge, she released them and placed her hands on the back of his neck, gently sifting through the thick white fur. Her touch sent sparks of electricity down his spine, lighting him up from the inside.

He never wanted her to stop.

She twined her fingers around the strands of hair at the base of his skull and gripped lightly, and Oswald simply *melted.* It was official. Whatever this goddess told him to do, he would do it. He belonged to her, body and soul.

"Oswald... is this okay with you?" Her voice was low and husky, her eyes meeting his.

He swallowed audibly as he gazed into those beautiful eyes. "Yes, *please.* Do whatever you want with me." The words came out rougher than normal as he fought to get them out. "Whatever you want."

Stefania's hands left his neck, trailing down through his chest fur as she replied a little breathlessly, "I think we should take it slow... but I want to touch you. And... I want you to touch me, too. If you'd like."

The paws he still had clenched around her hips spasmed at her words and she moaned, rocking slightly against him.

She was spectacular.

And then- she leaned down and lightly pressed her lips to his. He didn't think the vibrations in his chest could hum any faster than they already were, but they immediately shot to another level when she kissed him.

Her lips were so soft. Oswald had seen humans kiss on the television, and he tried to mimic the movements as best as his fangs allowed. She didn't seem to mind his inexperience as she continued to rock against him and run her hands all through his fur. His brain short-circuited as his world was reduced to the feeling of her mouth on his and her luscious body on his lap, the delicious taste of her invading every molecule of his soul. He trembled violently as he held himself in check. He couldn't unleash himself on her.

Not yet.

Not *this* time, the very first time he got to embrace her like this and feel her magnificent curves move against his. He would wait until she wanted him wild and untamed, begging for his knot. His mate.

His mate.

She slid her tongue against one of his fangs and his mouth parted for her on instinct.

He couldn't contain his cock any longer at the feeling of her slick tongue caressing his. It slid free of his body and Stefania gasped at the sudden feel of it. One of his paws was still clutching her hip, holding her in place as he thrust against her. He couldn't stop, couldn't stop, couldn't stop...

Stefania broke the kiss and glanced down to where they were grinding together. He heard her breath catch in her throat when she beheld his fully engorged cock, and a thread of doubt sluiced through him. Oswald didn't have any other yeti-folk around to compare against, but he figured he was an average yeti with an average yeti cock: long and thick, ending in a tapered point, and sporting the newly-activated knot bulging at its base.

He croaked out, "I am sorry, I cannot control it... you feel so amazing... is this okay?"

She scooted back on his thighs to examine it further. His mind whirled with the possibilities- every second of his past, present, and future seemed to hang on this moment. Was she disgusted? Turned off?

She smirked again and he couldn't stop from emitting a low whine of anticipation. And when she reached down and stroked him from root to tip with no hesitation, he barked out a growl of pure pleasure, his body arching up into hers.

Stefania braced her other hand on his shoulder and leaned over to murmur in his ear as she continued to work him. "Oh, Oswald, this is more than okay for me. Tell me if you want me to stop."

He shook his head frantically. "No, do not stop. Please."

She licked the fuzzy shell of his ear before whispering, "Good, then I won't. You're doing so, so good."

He grunted and gasped with each stroke, chest heaving as the pleasure coursed through his body. "Please... please, can I see you? Let me look at you, Stefania."

She paused her ministrations and Oswald groaned, hips unconsciously grinding into her hand, seeking the friction. She leaned back to look him in the eyes again. "But you've already seen me, Oswald. You saw all of me just a few days ago, spying on me while I was in the shower." Her fingertips lightly teased up and down his shaft. "I should make you wait for the privilege of seeing me up close."

He groaned again at her featherlight touch and began to babble out an apology. "I am so sorry. You are just so beautiful and I could not look away. Please, I will do anything you want me to do. Just let me see you, let me touch you. Please, Stefania, *please.*"

The last "please" came out slightly garbled as she squeezed his knot. "All right. Since you asked so nicely..." She trailed off as she released him and slid off of his lap.

Oswald's cock lamented her absence and he slid one of his paws over the tapered tip. Stefania shook her head before she peeled off her shirt.

"Oh, no. You're not allowed to come until I say you can, so be careful. Consider this your punishment for spying on me."

He growled in frustration but let go of himself and gripped the couch cushions as she slowly stripped for him. Of course he'd seen her gorgeous curves multiple times now, but now that she was three feet in front of him? He wanted to fall down and worship at her feet. She was the most exquisite thing he'd ever seen. Long, long legs. Hair the color of flames. Strong and soft. And *his.*

She settled back on his lap and gently took his paws in her hands, placing them on her breasts. They were so *soft* and he just couldn't believe this was happening. His cock began to drip as she resumed stroking him. His stunning mate, naked and moaning in his lap? He wasn't going to last long.

"Before you come, I want you to make *me* come, Oswald. Can you do that for me?"

Oswald nodded, beyond words. Her words were low and hypnotic, and he was pretty sure he'd jump off a cliff if she asked him to.

"Good. Go ahead... touch me. Do you know much about the anatomy of human women?"

He shook his head and she took a paw from where he'd been kneading her breast and lowered it to the thatch of hair at the apex of her thighs, showing him what to do. She was warm and wet and ready for him and he wanted to do nothing more than to shove his cock into her over and over-

But instead, he kept himself tightly leashed as he rubbed her slick core with his knuckles, focusing on the top as she instructed him, watching her carefully to see what she liked best. She writhed on top of him, grinding and stroking him mercilessly as she neared her climax. He couldn't last much longer.

"Fuck, Oswald, that's good. Yes, just like that- please don't stop, don't stop, don't stop. You're so good at this. Right... there... *fuck, yes, Oswald!*"

Stefania shattered over him with a scream, her thighs clenching around his and her strokes of his cock becoming stuttered and uneven. It didn't matter- hearing her cries and seeing her come undone was enough, and he growled and begged her to let him come as he bucked against her hand.

"Stefania, I cannot hold... *please...*"

She finally relented, her words coming out in gasps as she rode out the waves of her orgasm. "Yes, Oswald, you can come. You did such an amazing job. Come for me. Let go for me."

His brain went blank as intense pleasure radiated through him and he growled and shuddered against her, reveling in her praise as he spurted all over the both of them.

Drained, Oswald slumped on the couch, Stefania once again gently sifting her hands through his fur as he continued to shake with minor aftershocks. She grinned at him as he stared at her in astonishment. "You did so good, darling Oswald. You made me come *so* hard."

He wrapped his arms around her and held her to him, not caring that they were both covered in his release. She jolted in surprise at the sudden hug, but she settled into it and put her head in the crook of his neck.

He closed his eyes and breathed deeply, trying to work through the sudden onslaught of feelings that barreled through his chest. She felt like everything he'd ever wanted.

She felt like home.

They stayed like that for a long time, wrapped around each

other.

Long after his cock was sheathed and the vibrations in his chest finally calmed down to a reasonable rumble, Stefania lifted her head and gently kissed Oswald's cheek. "I don't know about you, but I think I'd like a shower and a nap."

He reluctantly released her and studied her face for any signs of regret. There didn't seem to be any. Was she truly fine with what they had just done? And if so... when could they do that again? "I like that idea as well."

When she slid off his lap, he brought one of his blue-grey knuckles up to his face and licked it, suppressing a moan at her delectable taste. This round, she had called the shots- but if she let him do this again, he was going to devour her.

She held out her hand, and he took it to follow her to the bathroom.

He'd follow her anywhere.

Chapter 13

Stefania

The next morning, Stefania woke and leisurely stretched her arms above her head, snuggling further into the blankets. It was the Friday morning after Thanksgiving and *thank*fully she had the day off of work.

Thanksgiving...

She gasped and clutched a pillow to her chest as the memories of yesterday flooded in. Cooking all day. Tromping out into the woods. Inviting Oswald to dinner. Being carried by Oswald all the way from his cabin. Enjoying lively conversation and good company. Relaxing on the couch.

Straddling Oswald.

Kissing Oswald.

Feeling Oswald's hands everywhere.

Showering with Oswald afterwards.

Stefania's entire body flushed as she relived every moment of her domination of the gentle yeti. She usually preferred her partners to take charge in the bedroom, but he'd been like putty in her hands and the feeling of complete control over this giant creature was unlike anything she'd ever felt before. He made her feel strong, powerful, and cherished. He didn't demand anything of her, instead accepting whatever she felt like giving.

And she felt like giving him everything.

Afterwards hadn't been awkward like many of her past experiences, either. They had soaped each other up in the giant stall, Oswald running reverent fingers over her entire body. Judging by the way his hands lingered in certain areas, she had a feeling he was fighting the desire to initiate a second round. However, he seemed happily content to enjoy her company in the rainfall shower, which he fit under even while standing at his full height of over seven feet. She couldn't imagine how difficult it was for him to bathe in the much smaller stall of his cabin.

Maybe she'd invite him to come over and use the shower for the rest of the time she lived here. (*Maybe I'll join him in it.*) And when he shook himself like a dog to get rid of the excess water before toweling off- it was the cutest thing she'd ever seen.

When they were dry, he tucked her into the big bed, gave her a soft forehead nuzzle, and left. She had almost asked him to stay with her, but she needed space to process everything that had transpired between them.

Had it really only been less than a week since she'd first met Oswald? If she didn't still have lingering soreness from her terrifying river adventure, she could've convinced herself that it had already been months.

Stefania threw off the comforter and padded into the bathroom, thoughts in a turmoil. She didn't regret anything of the events of last night, but she didn't know quite what to think. She'd had a sexual encounter with a cryptid! He was a creature that wasn't supposed to exist- but here he was, in the flesh. A walking, talking yeti.

She needed to speak to him soon about selling the house before this went any further. (She'd ignored several calls from Gary Klein this week- the agent did not take no for an answer. If this was any indication of how he treated his relationships, it was a massive red flag.) If Oswald formed an attachment to her, what would happen when she left? Would he try to follow her to Seattle? The city was clearly no place for a yeti.

He'd held her so tightly last night that she still felt that hug in her soul. This sweet, thoughtful creature was indeed isolated out here. What if she introduced him to Henry to see if Henry could look after him?

She snorted to herself. Physically, a seven-foot-tall musclebound yeti did not need anyone to look after it.

Although... being Charles' closest friend, maybe Henry already knows of Oswald's existence? Surely he would've warned her if he knew of Oswald, but she rationalized that Henry knew she wasn't staying. Why would he bother mentioning a secret tenant when she was going to be selling the place?

Plus, she wouldn't have believed Henry anyway. *A yeti? Surely you jest! Come on, let's get you to a psychiatrist.*

She checked the front porch to see if there were any new packages on her stoop. Sure enough, one sat on the doormat, wrapped in the same old newspaper as the others. Stefania peeled back the newspaper to discover an intricately carved wooden bracelet with the words *mērō muṭu* inscribed on the inside in small block letters.

A quick search on the internet revealed that the words meant "my heart" in Nepali. Stefania's own heart beat a little faster. This seemed to confirm her suspicions that the gifts were from Oswald, as yeti-folk were from Nepal. If it was indeed from Oswald... was he getting too attached too fast? Was she going to break his heart when she told him she was moving back to Seattle?

She slid the thin bracelet onto her wrist and admired the beautiful design. The inscription looked freshly carved- in fact, the entire bracelet looked and smelled like it had just been finished. If it was as fresh as she thought it was, then this piece of jewelry could not have been made by Charles.

But if this bracelet was from Oswald, where had he gotten it? Had he stolen it from a store or some roadside booth and added the inscription himself? The tiny letters were neat and even, and her graphic design brain appreciated the perfect kerning of the text. If Oswald had managed to add that inscription so precisely, then it was possible that he had the skill to carve other things as well.

Stefania gazed around the living room of the house, looking at the space in a new light. Was *Oswald* the one who had painstakingly etched designs into the door frames of this cabin? Was *Oswald* the one who had carved all of the figurines that Ana sold at Winterhaven Market? That envelope full of cash labeled with Oswald's name- were those earnings from the sales?

Her mind whirring, Stefania walked into the dining room and stared at *The Hug* statue. Her favorite carving of them all that embodied the sense of hope, belonging, and love that one feels when they've found their match... had probably been carved by a yeti.

A lonely, sequestered yeti with an artist's soul.

Determination settled into Stefania's bones. She only had two more weeks in Alaska, but she could use her remaining time to grant Oswald as much affection and happiness as possible.

Stefania was just about to heat up some Thanksgiving leftovers for an early dinner when the distinct sound of a snowmobile roared down the driveway.

Oswald had been absent all day, and she hoped he wasn't freaked out from the events of yesterday. If she didn't see him by Sunday, she'd trek back out to his cabin and make him talk to her. Now that she knew approximately where it was, she figured she could find it again.

She opened the front door to see two people dismounting from a gleaming black and silver snowmobile. The passenger was clad in all pink winter gear, while the driver was bundled up in solid black. It took her a second to recognize Bridget and Ana thanks to all the layers of puffy clothing. Stefania grinned, delighted to see them. "Well, hey! What are you two doing here?"

Bridget pushed her pink goggles onto her helmet and lowered the scarf from around the bottom half of her face. "Ana wanted to test out her fancy new snowmobile so I suggested we ride out here to see if you were up for a movie night!"

Ana removed her gloves and unzipped a coat pocket, pulling out a DVD case. "We brought Pride and Prejudice! The 2005 version, not the 1995. We need more time on another day to devote to Colin Firth."

Bridget pretended to swoon into the snow. "I just can't pick a favorite Mr. Darcy. They're all my favorite."

Stefania laughed. "I couldn't agree with you more! Come on in. I was just about to have some leftovers for dinner- are either of you hungry?"

The two ladies picked their way through the snow to the porch as Bridget replied, "Yes please, I'm famished! Beans was closed today and I wanted a day off from cooking. All I've eaten today is one measly bowl of cereal. Feed me, please!"

Ana fondly rolled her eyes at Bridget's dramatics and waved a hand at the side of the yard. "Your snowman is huge! How did you manage to build one so big?"

"What? I haven't built..." Stefania trailed off as she spotted the enormous snowman in her yard, smiling merrily at her between two pine trees. From the porch, it looked like it was at least ten feet tall. "What on earth? Who...?"

Oswald. It had to be. Was this what he'd been doing all day? Nobody else could possibly be strong enough to build a snowman of that size without the help of a machine. Even a team of professional strongmen probably wouldn't be able to construct something like that. She knew Oswald was strong, but this was beyond impressive.

Her stomach fluttered at the thought of all that strength. *I can't believe I had all those muscles under me last night.*

She laughed weakly, trying to recover. "Must've been some of the construction workers that were here this week. I can't believe I didn't notice it, but I've been staying inside after last weekend's debacle."

She didn't like lying to her two new friends, but what choice did she have? She didn't know them well enough yet to let them in on the secret. She couldn't break Oswald's trust.

Ana glanced over at Stefania, the skepticism clear in her expression. "Must've been some strong construction workers. That thing is massive."

"Adorable, though!" Bridget chimed in. "He's such a happy snowman. I think they must have a crush on you."

A low growl emanated from behind the snowman, just loud enough for all three women to hear. Heat flushed through Stefania's cheeks. *Oh crap, Oswald's out there right now. I have to get them inside!*

Stefania herded her friends into the house before anyone could comment on the growl. "I'm freezing, come on in! It *is* cute, and I absolutely love it! Whoever made it is seriously talented. Many thanks to them!"

She shut the door with one last glance outside at the giant jolly snowman.

Stefania couldn't remember the last time she'd had a movie night with friends. They ate leftovers, lounged under warm blankets, and collectively swooned over Matthew MacFadyen as Mr. Darcy. She felt herself relaxing more and more as the evening wore on, reveling in the feeling of contentment of being able to be herself around the two women. She wasn't completely alone and friendless in Seattle- she had acquaintances that she occasionally met up with, but she wasn't necessarily close to any of them. And she did have her old college friends, but they were scattered across the globe, grown apart by time and space.

There was something to be said for having a group of friends that could just show up your house and relax with you- no expectations, no fancy clothes, no need to pretend to be perfectly put together.

What a relief to just be yourself and be accepted as you are.

Ana and Bridget left later that evening, despite Stefania's fear of them traveling back to town in the dark on a snowmobile. Ana, who had been born and raised in Winterhaven, just scoffed and said she could drive the route with her eyes closed. Bridget, trusting as always, had climbed on the back of the black snowmobile without reservation. Stefania watched as they made their way through the pitch-black forest, taillights swallowed up by the dark. Was Oswald still out there or had he gone back to his cabin for the night?

A wicked thought crossed her mind. *If he's out there, I bet I can make him come running.*

Stefania left the front door unlocked and made her way to the bathroom, the plan formulating in her mind. Nothing appeared to be outside of the big bathroom window, but she slowly stripped anyways, throwing a little extra slink into her moves in case he was watching. She had just bent over to slip off her underwear when she heard it- a low whine from outside.

She smiled to herself. So he *was* watching.

Stefania finished her sultry striptease and stepped into the shower, turning on the water. While she waited for it to heat up, she shook her hair out from her braid, letting the coppery tresses fall down to her lower back before gathering it back up into a bun. She'd seen the way Oswald looked at her hair- he loved it.

She peeked at the window over her shoulder. He wasn't visible at the window yet... she'd have to do better.

She repeated her actions from Tuesday that had gotten him so worked up that he'd scratched the window- but this time, she put more intention into the act as she performed for her yeti. She used slower, more sensual touches as she brought herself to the edge over and over again, but she held off on her climax as she waited for him. As she neared each peak, she'd moan his name and was satisfied to hear the answering growls from outside the window. When she stopped, he whined in protest.

She had just paused again when she heard a frustrated bark, followed by complete silence. Stefania glanced towards the glass and didn't see those glacial eyes that had been so fixated on her- had he got fed up and left?

She didn't have much time to wonder. Oswald burst into the bathroom and stormed over to the shower, his expression blazing with need. Without hesitation, he reached under her thighs and picked her up, slamming her back against the shower wall as her legs automatically draped over his shoulders. She didn't have any time to mentally thank the architect of this bathroom for high ceilings before Oswald buried his face between her legs.

And then, he *feasted*.

Stefania, already at the precipice of an orgasm, cried and shuddered with pleasure as he ravenously devoured her. She hadn't expected to feel the added vibration from his thrumming chest, but he was purring so strongly that it rattled up his throat and radiated into her core. Her head fell back against the shower tiles as her hands grasped at the soft fur of his head.

A fang grazed her clit and the pleasure crested, bliss shooting through her body in waves.

Oswald continued feasting as she shook through her climax, until it was too much to bear. She grabbed his horns, causing him to immediately freeze.

"Too... sensitive," she panted out.

She didn't want to admit it, but she enjoyed knowing that grabbing his highly sensitive horns would make him stop in his tracks. It was like he had an *off* button.

Her knees almost buckled when he set her down and he wrapped his arms around her to keep her steady, rubbing his claws gently up and down her back. He leaned down to drop a kiss the top of her head and his deep voice rumbled in her ear from where she was pressed against his chest. "Are you all right?"

She giggled helplessly. "I just edged myself for what felt like an eternity, and it was totally worth it. I'm doing *great.*"

His throaty laugh echoed throughout the shower and he hugged her tighter, making his unsheathed cock press against her stomach. She pulled away from his chest and glanced down at it. Yesterday's foray had been a blur and her mind hadn't really processed what he was packing.

Oswald's cock was unlike anything she'd ever seen before.

Her mouth watered a little bit at the sight of it. It was long, thick, tapered, and the same blue-grey as his hands and face, with a slight bulge at the base. The bulge intrigued her- she had read enough monster romances to realize just what that protrusion might be. While the rest of it looked manageable, she was a little worried about how that bulge would fit inside a human woman.

She stroked a hand down his length to the base, reveling in his full-body shudder at her touch. "Oswald... is this a knot?"

Chapter 14

Oswald

Oswald stared down at Stefania, her small hand caressing his cock. Berries and vanilla filled his nostrils and the taste of her coated his tongue. He could've held her up against that wall for hours if she'd let him.

She'd teased him on purpose just to get him in here, and he couldn't be happier for it.

What a lucky yeti he was.

He groaned as she lightly squeezed his knot. "That is my knot, yes." The *yes* was gasped as she raked her fingernails across it, sending sparks of pleasure down to his toes. He wouldn't last long if she kept that up. Would she even let him come right away, or would she edge him just as long as she had edged herself?

Even thinking about the potential for delayed or denied gratification made his balls draw up, readying for the inevitable. *Talk about irony.*

She didn't make him wait long. Instead, she slid down to her knees and wasted no time taking him into her mouth, leaving him to clutch blindly at the shower tiles as wave after wave of ecstasy pumped through his veins. How was it possible to feel so *good*?

Despite his claws scrabbling mindlessly at the walls, Oswald kept his hips still. He didn't want to hurt her with his girth, but when she finally grabbed his thighs and urged him to move against her face?

He didn't need to be told twice.

He knew he wasn't going to last. She was so warm and wet and when she hollowed out her cheeks and sucked him to the back of her throat, he begged her to let him come. She merely looked up at him through her lashes, then nodded and squeezed his knot hard. He sucked in a breath as intense pleasure raced through him, zeroing in on his groin.

At the very last second, he pulled out of her mouth and spilled himself all over her perfect breasts, a guttural grunt escaping with every spurt of his cock. Small tremors rippled through his body for a few moments until he mentally collected himself and stared down at her, wide-eyed.

In the course of two days, she'd shown him more intimacy than he'd had in his entire life.

His mate looked thoroughly satisfied with herself, running a finger through the mess he'd left on her chest as she smirked up at him. "Did you enjoy that?"

Oswald wheezed out a laugh and extended a paw to help her up. "You are a devilish minx of a woman. You know exactly what you do to me."

"Yes, but I like to hear the words directly from the source."

He directed her back under the shower spray and gently wiped at her chest, taking a few extra moments to caress each breast. He didn't miss the hitch in her breath or the arch in her back when he lightly brushed over her nipples.

He leaned down to murmur into her ear. She wanted words? He'd give them to her. "Simply put, my sweet Stefania... you enthrall me. I am at your utter mercy."

His claws continued carefully tracing designs on her chest. She swayed against him, eyelids going heavy and hands clutching his sides for support. In the back of his mind, he noted that the water was beginning to turn from hot to lukewarm. While it wouldn't affect him, he didn't want his mate to go through another traumatizing bout with cold water.

"Every bit of you is perfection." A tweak of her sensitive nipple with his claw drew a gasp from her lips. "You have bewitched me, body and soul."

Stefania's gaze sharpened and snapped to his. "You were listening to Pride and Prejudice tonight?"

Oswald smiled at her. "I could not hear it, but this is not the first time I have seen this film. Your friend Ana hosts a regular outdoor movie night next to the Market during the fall and projects them onto a large screen. I am quite fond of that particular movie. She shows it at least once a year."

"How on earth has no one noticed a yeti at a movie night?"

He ran his claws down to her curvy hips and gave them a squeeze. "I stay very far away, up in a tree, and it is always dark by that time of the evening. Humans really only see what they want to see, and they are all focused on the screen. I am very careful, do not worry."

She grabbed handfuls of his chest fur, glaring up at him in mock-defiance. "You had better be careful. I can't even think of what might happen if the world discovers you. You are too sweet to be exposed to the world outside of Winterhaven."

Oswald growled and backed Stefania against the shower wall. He nuzzled into her neck, breathing her in and enjoying how much her pulse was racing- not out of fear, he knew, but out of excitement and lust. Lust for *him*. "I like you being as protective of me as I am of you."

He trailed a paw down the front of her stomach, and an idea popped into his head. He had to be so careful with his claws considering how fragile her skin was, and he was tired of not being able to touch her like he wanted to.

With a quick bite of his sharp fangs, the claw sheared clean off and he spat it out to the side of the shower. "I will clean these up later."

Stefania gasped. "What are you doing?"

"They will grow back." He bit off another one. "I want to be able to feel how tight you are with more than just my tongue." He took the rest of the claws off of his right paw in quick succession then immediately cupped between her thighs, a finger pad slipping over her clit before plunging into her core.

She let out a little scream of surprise and writhed against the wall. "Oh, fuck, Oswald! Holy shit!"

Just like her mouth, she was warm, wet, and so *tight* against his thick finger, and he knew she was going to feel magnificent wrapped around his cock. He curled his other arm around her waist, holding her up as he fucked her relentlessly with his finger.

Soon. He needed to have his cock in her soon.

His thumb brushed her clit and she whimpered and shuddered against him in response. So he did it again, and again, and again, until she convulsed around him with a long, drawn-out moan.

Oswald was rather proud at how fast he was picking this up.

Oswald nervously clutched the wooden comb in his paw as he stepped into the bedroom. He was going to do it- he was going to ask Stefania to brush out his fur. She wouldn't understand the significance- that brushing was a highly personal, intimate act that only a yeti's mate was allowed to perform- but he could explain that later. He kept telling himself that he *wanted* complete honesty between them... just not yet.

Stefania was already in bed, sitting up against the headboard. Her porcelain features glowed in the soft light of the bedside lamp, and she smiled shyly at Oswald while she flicked a strand of damp hair off of one shoulder. "I don't know if this is too forward, but would you like to stay the night? It's late and cold, and this bed is big enough for the two of us."

His chest picked up speed at the thought of spending the night wrapped around her, and he nodded enthusiastically. "I want to stay with you, as much as you will have me. You might regret inviting me in if you wake up sweating, though."

She laughed. "It won't be the first time we've shared a bed and I didn't mind the heat then, either. At least there's no threat of hypothermia this time."

He sat on the edge of the bed beside her and she reached out automatically to rub a hand down his arm. He basked in the familiarity of the touch. "Would you mind brushing out my fur before I get into bed? I do not shed much, but it will help reduce any potential hairs in your sheets."

"Of course. Will you braid my hair when I'm done? You did such a great job on it last time."

He smiled and handed her the comb he'd carved for her, thankful that he'd had the presence of mind to set it on the dresser before joining his mate in the shower. "Yes, of course. It might be a clumsier attempt without all of my claws, but I will try."

Stefania began, and Oswald was consumed by the waves of utter bliss that washed over him. It was one thing to comb yourself, but when someone else did it for you? Infinitely better. His skin tingled with each pass of the comb through his fur and his chest settled into a deep rolling purr.

He understood now, why only mates were allowed to groom each other- the sheer intimacy of the act was not meant to be shared with anyone else. As a yetling, his parents had occasionally needed to brush out his hard-to-reach places, but it was always done with businesslike efficiency- it wasn't meant to spark any feelings of love or contentment.

This... this was everything his heart could've ever desired.

They had been sitting in silence for several minutes, Stefania concentrating on the task at hand, when she spoke up. "Can I ask a question?" When he nodded, she continued. "Why don't you use contractions in your speech? You know, instead of saying 'I will' or 'do not', you could say 'I'll' or 'don't'. Is there a specific reason?"

Oswald shrugged, a purely human move that he'd adopted from Charles. "English is not my first language, and my mouth is not shaped as yours is. Some of the words are very hard for me to pronounce with fangs, and forming complete sentences can be difficult. I have to choose my words with care, and it is easier for me to treat each word separately rather than try to meld them together. Is it... wrong?"

"No, not at all- that makes perfect sense. I was just wondering, that's all. Your speech pattern reminded me of an android from a sci-fi TV show that also spoke as you do. I like it." She sat up on her knees and ran the comb between his horns. He closed his eyes and barely repressed a full-body shudder of pleasure at the sensation of the comb on his scalp.

After a few moments he asked, "Is there anything else you would like to know?"

She sifted through the soft fur on his back with delicate hands. "I'd like to know much more about you. You've given me some of your backstory and I've enjoyed learning all about yeti culture. And since we've... become better acquainted..." At Stefania's pause, he cracked an eye open and turned to glance at her. She was blushing furiously.

"Yes?"

She cleared her throat and returned to combing out some of the fur on his shoulder. "I know that you haven't had experience with human women and there are no yeti-folk around here... so you are a virgin, right?"

Oswald let out a surprised laugh. "The concept of virginity does not exist for yeti-folk, but no, I have not had the opportunity to be with a female before. Or any other gender, for that matter, as some yeti-folk do not prescribe to one or the other."

He left out the fact that almost all yeti-folk mated for life.

"Do you think you would ever want to go back to Nepal and find a yeti life-partner? Have a wife and make cute yeti babies?"

He twisted around to face her fully. "No, my sweet Stefania. My life is here in Alaska." *My mate is here in Alaska.* "I do not wish to leave."

Stefania's eyes met his. "Oh… I just wondered. It seems like it would get lonely up here. You must want some sort of companionship."

He shrugged again. "I cannot lie, I have often longed for a mate to keep me company during the long winter nights. But I am happy with how life has turned out for me thus far."

"And what do you do to keep busy during the long winter nights? Is there… a hobby you enjoy?"

She stopped brushing and held up the comb, grinning.

Alarm bells went off in Oswald's head and he momentarily forgot to breathe. She'd figured it out. She knew all of the gifts had been coming from him, knew he was the one who had carved every single one.

It was time to come clean about the origin of the gifts, but he'd still keep the fact that they were meant as courting gifts to himself. It didn't feel like the right time.

"I have a small carving workshop next to my cabin. When I was injured, Charles noticed that I liked to carve little designs with my claws. He gave me my first set of tools and the rest is history." Oswald sighed. "He encouraged me to pursue woodworking and even let me add decorations throughout the house, as you can see. I worked on the door frames as a part of therapy to practice standing for longer and longer periods of time."

She laid a comforting hand on his shoulder. "I'm so sorry he's gone. I know you must miss him dearly. But Oswald, why didn't you tell me that all of the carvings were made by you? Have you been leaving them on my doorstep all this time?"

He ran a paw over his face, slightly embarrassed. How was he supposed to explain this? But Stefania continued on, saving him the trouble. "And the statue on my dining room table- *The Hug*- you made that?"

He nodded.

"It's so much different that your other pieces. What was the motivation for that one?"

Oswald swallowed hard. "It is a personal piece and was never meant to go to the Market. After I made it, Charles came by to collect a few things to sell and accidentally took that one with him. I did not realize it was gone right away, and when I noticed its absence, Charles had become bedridden. There was no way for me to get the statue back- I could only hope that someone would find it and cherish it as much as I did."

A glimmer of tears began to show in Stefania's eyes. "You should've said something the first day you came in. I would've given it back to you. You can take it home tomorrow!"

He laid a paw over her hand. "I think it has found its rightful home- it is yours now. When I carved it, I was feeling very sad and alone… and yet hopeful that one day I would feel that special connection with another being. In just a few days, you have given me the gift of that connection. Please keep it, and think of the joy you have given me whenever you see it."

She threw her arms around him and they held each other for a long, long time.

Chapter 15

Stefania

For the second time in a week, Stefania woke up in the warm cocoon of furry white arms. The heat pumping off of the yeti's big body coupled with the steady rumble of his purr threatened to lull her back into slumber, but she carefully rolled over to face him. He was awake, smiling gently down at her. She could practically see hearts in his eyes and her own heart seized with guilt in response.

How am I going to tell him that I'm not staying when he looks at me like I hung the moon?

His voice was a quiet rumble. "Good morning, *mērō muṭu*. How did you sleep?"

She yawned and belatedly clapped a hand over her mouth. "I'm sure I have morning breath, sorry. I slept great. What about you?"

His yawn matched her own, and she marveled at the sheer number of sharp teeth he possessed. And no morning breath. It wasn't fair. "I have never had a better night's sleep in my life."

She settled against him, using his meaty arm as a pillow. A

quick flashback of last night's stunning display of strength in the shower made her shiver involuntarily. "Really? Never?"

"No."

"It's probably this fancy mattress."

Oswald curled an arm around her, drawing her even closer. "No. Being next to you made it the best night of my life."

Stefania melted just a little more. He was such a sweet yeti, and was clearly lonely- why wouldn't he want to go back to Nepal and find himself a nice yeti partner? He had mentioned last night that his life was here in Alaska, but what a solitary life it seemed to be.

She closed her eyes, and they lay in contented silence for a while before Oswald spoke again. "What are your plans for today?"

"No plans, really. The Saturday after Thanksgiving used to be the day that we would go pick out a Christmas tree every year, but..." She trailed off.

He prodded her gently. "But what?"

"I haven't gotten a Christmas tree in a long time. I haven't really been in the holiday spirit since my mother passed. It was her favorite time of year, and I just... miss her so much. I *want* to honor her memory and keep the traditions alive, but I couldn't seem to do it alone. And my ex-" she paused, thinking of how to describe Doug. "My ex told me that nothing would ever be as good as his mother's holiday decorations, and it felt useless to even try. I didn't want to feel like I was competing with her for his attention and approval, so I just never bothered." She rolled her eyes. "That alone should've been a massive red flag."

Oswald growled darkly and rubbed a possessive hand down her arm. He'd been touching her a lot more freely since last night- she could tell that he was enjoying having the ability to touch her without worrying about his claws piercing her delicate flesh.

"Besides," she continued, trying to lighten the mood, "I don't have any ornaments here, so it would just be a bare tree."

131

He smiled. "Have you not gone through the garage yet? Charles had a few boxes of decorations that he made me fetch for him every holiday season. If you want a tree, my sweet Stefania, I can get you a tree."

Her heart cracked a little in her chest, and she tried to keep the waver out of her voice as she whispered, "You would get me a tree?"

With a half-shrug he replied, "Of course. I got one for Charles every year. Let me get one for you, *mērō muṭu*. Let me make this Christmas special for you."

Her nose stung as tears formed in her eyes. *That might be the sweetest thing anyone has ever done for me in my adult life.* She tried to surreptitiously wipe her face. "I'd like that very much, Oswald. Thank you."

Oswald seemed to note the change in her demeanor and pulled her up so she was laying on top of him. His shoulders were basically the width of a twin-size bed, and once again she felt downright minuscule on top of his muscular frame. She buried her face in his chest, concentrating on his rhythmic breathing.

He squeezed her tightly but didn't speak, allowing her the time and space to work out her emotions. When she had a handle on herself, Stefania asked, "You've called me *mērō muṭu* several times and it's inscribed on the bracelet you left me- does it have a special significance?"

His voice seemed even deeper with her cheek pressed against his chest. "It is a term of endearment within the yeti-folk community." He swallowed heavily. "It is what my parents called each other."

She raised her head and stared up at his glacial blue eyes. Sorrow lined his features, and she was reminded that she was not the only one that harbored bone-deep grief. But they were not alone, and she could give him all of herself in the short time that she had left in Alaska. She could give him a new memory of a happier holiday.

"All right, Oswald. Let's decorate a tree today."

That afternoon, Oswald disappeared for an hour before returning with a beautiful fir tree. It was almost flawless, with only a slight bend in the top of the trunk that Stefania found endearing. She proclaimed that the tree was absolutely perfect, and Oswald practically glowed in her praise.

She made soup and sandwiches for their dinner while Oswald hauled in all of the decorations, and they spent the rest of the evening watching Christmas movies and trimming the tree.

And as they hung each ornament while Bing Crosby crooned in the background about jingle bells, a piece of Stefania's heart seemed to knit itself back together.

Time flew by over the next week. The days were a blur of renovations, the nights a blur of orgasms delivered by yeti. They settled into a comfortable routine, with Oswald staying with her every night and reluctantly slinking out at the crack of dawn before the construction crew arrived. Stefania got the sense that he was never far from the house and just lurked in the surrounding woods all day. The moment that the last crew truck took off down her driveway, her yeti would appear and sweep her off her feet.

The Monday morning after Thanksgiving, Henry had taken one look at the giant snowman in the yard and narrowed his eyes thoughtfully, making Stefania suspicious. Did Henry know about Oswald? She couldn't figure out a way to bring it up in conversation. If she asked Henry about yeti-folk in the area and he didn't know of Oswald's existence, she'd come off looking like a raving lunatic.

Have you seen a giant white yeti in the area? Whittles wood for a living, lives on the property, speaks English with a cute lisp? No? Oh, okay. Never mind...

Henry would probably look at her like she had two heads.

He was at the cabin with his crew every day, keeping track of the construction progress and often repairing random items that weren't even on the crew's punch list. She'd caught him fixing a squeaky hinge on the bathroom door, caulking the guest tub, and stabilizing the living room ceiling fan, among a multitude of other things.

When she scolded him for doing all this extra work, he just laughed and told her he'd always offered to fix these things for Charles. Charles had always refused, saying he felt like asking for repair work was taking advantage of Henry's kindness and skill. "I always told him that it's not taking advantage of me if I offer!" Henry proclaimed. "But Charles was firm about making me sit and enjoy myself whenever I came over."

Charles himself remained an enigma. Henry regaled her with stories of lively backgammon matches and Thanksgiving dinners, but she still couldn't ascertain why no one in her family had ever mentioned him. *What could he have done that was so horrible?*

She'd searched the house again and again, and there were no more clues. It seemed that Charles's past was going to remain an unsolved mystery.

A month had flown by since she'd first arrived in Winterhaven, and the house now looked just as Stefania had envisioned. The kitchen was finally finished, the porch had been stained and sealed, new blinds were hung, and bit by bit she executed step five of her grand plan. The cabin was close to everything she had wanted in a home, and she hoped whoever bought it would love it as much as she did.

What she had originally viewed as a simple flip job had become a labor of love, and the cabin now felt like her perfect sanctuary. A month in Alaska had also changed her- she had found close friends in Bridget and Ana, a father figure in Henry, and a surprisingly attentive lover in Oswald.

She realized that she really didn't miss Seattle at all. No bouts of homesickness, no yearning to go back into the office.

Working remotely suited her and she had taken over Charles' office as her own workspace. If she stayed here, she could swap out the old rickety desk with a more modern standing desk and purchase a more comfortable chair. Maybe she could get a dog as a companion to keep her company while she worked- there was a spot in the corner that would be perfect for a dog bed. Did Oswald like dogs? Would he want a pet?

She shook off the adorable image that floated through her mind of Oswald curled up contentedly around a sleepy dog. She wasn't staying here. That wasn't part of the plan. Oswald, Bridget, Ana, Henry- none of them had been part of the plan.

After the house was ready to be put on the market, only one step remained in her list: *Be home by Christmas and start the new year with a clean slate.*

Maybe once she was back in Seattle, she'd try harder at making friends- real friends that she could be herself around. She could try harder to find a partner to share life with- someone who was kind, generous, patient, affectionate, strong. Someone who protected her heart and her body and looked at her like she hung the moon.

Someone like Oswald.

Chapter 16

Stefania

In mid-December, everything came crashing down around her.

Kim, the real estate agent, had brought a photographer by yesterday to take pictures of the house for the listing, all the while nodding her approval of the changes and telling Stefania that she had missed her calling as an interior designer. Stefania had quietly preened at the compliment and looked at the cabin with fresh perspective and a sense of pride. She had done it- she had successfully renovated a home. Did she have a lot of outside help in making it happen? Definitely. Had she spent a substantial portion of her inheritance to get the cabin exactly how she wanted? Also, yes.

Was she proud of herself for being brave and taking the leap? Absolutely.

Stefania sat on a barstool at the kitchen island, carefully checking the photos Kim had emailed over this morning and giggling when she saw faint traces of Oswald in some of the exterior shots. The clues would never be noticed if a person wasn't specifically looking for them, but she had become so familiar with her yeti that she could pick out a hint of a horn peeking from behind a tree or a not-quite-covered footprint in the snow. He was as much a part of this property as the house itself.

The yeti himself snuggled up behind her, wrapping his burly arms around her waist and resting his chin on her shoulder. It was a Friday and she had no plans for the day besides work, so he had lingered in the house longer than usual. Oswald had spent every night of the last two weeks in her bed, both of them enjoying each other as much as possible. They had never taken it to the next step- and though he gave every indication that he was more than willing to take it further, he never pushed or asked her for more.

Her time with Oswald had taught her a lot about herself. She never before considered herself a dominant lover, but something about having the power to make this massive creature beg for release gave her a new sense of deep satisfaction. He wished for nothing more than to please her, and in turn, she wanted nothing more than to make all of his wishes come true. Though her extensive reading of smut gave her an idea of how to dominate him in a respectful and loving way, she had dived into further research over the past two weeks, poring through multiple e-books on the subject of topping to make sure that she was meeting his needs with appropriate consent and aftercare.

Oswald's preferred aftercare? Anything that included having her hands on him, as he was a tactile being and easily turned to mush in her hands. At the top of that list was showering, brushing his fur out, and cuddling until they fell asleep- or until one of them initiated another round.

But she didn't dominate him all the time- in fact, each night was different and unpredictable, and Stefania loved it. Sometimes Oswald came in and immediately ravaged her, while other nights they would have dinner and cuddle on the couch for hours, just talking about anything and everything. He had such a genuine curiosity about herself and the world as a whole, and she found their conversations deeply refreshing.

As their connection grew deeper, she found herself dreading the inevitable conversation about going back to Seattle. More than ever, she didn't want to hurt him.

"What are you looking at, *mērō mu ṭu*?"

She leaned back against him and reached up to run a hand down his fuzzy cheek. She loved the sheer size of him, loved feeling downright dainty next to his enormous stature.

The doorbell rang, saving Stefania from answering. Oswald immediately unwound his arms from her waist and straightened, preparing to dash out the back door. She stopped him with a hand on his arm.

"I'm not expecting anyone today. I'll go see who it is, just stay in the kitchen. I'll be right back."

She padded to the front door and unlocked it. On the other side of the door stood a man a few inches shorter than her, with sandy blonde hair combed over his balding forehead and brown eyes so bloodshot that she figured he was either hungover or high. "Stefania Clarke?"

Stefania leaned against the doorway, instantly on alert. "Can I help you?"

The man raised himself to his full height, a move designed to either impress or intimidate her. It did neither, and she barely hid her growing disdain as she stared down at him. "I'm Gary Klein of Klein Realty. I've been trying to reach you for a while now about selling your property, Mrs. Clarke. Is your husband around so I can talk to him?"

His eyes landed on her chest and stayed there for a few lingering moments.

Stefania straightened and crossed her arms over her chest. The utter gall of this man. *This* was the infamous Gary Klein? *How could Ana have even dated this guy?* "I'm not married, so you'll have to deal directly with me. As I told you before, I'm not interested in your services."

Gary was not deterred in the slightest. "I know you have Kim as your current agent, but I can get you much better offers on the property than she can. I can sell this place in twenty-four hours, and I've got men in my network who would pay cash for this house as-is, thousands over the asking price. Kim won't be able to get you anything like that."

Something clattered in the kitchen, and her heart dropped in her sternum. Had Oswald heard that?

She contemplated stepping outside and shutting the door, but she wasn't dressed for the frigid temperatures. The wind was slicing through her thin pajamas even now, causing her to shiver. She needed to get rid of this Gary Klein immediately.

"Mr. Klein- "

He cut her off by holding up a hand to stop her. "Please, sweetheart, call me Gary."

She ground her teeth together and tried again. "Fine. *Gary*, I've already entered into an agreement with Kim, so I don't need your help. Now, I've got work to do- have a great day."

She started to close the door, but Gary's arm shot out to hold it open. Her face heated as she glared daggers at this misogynistic asshole. Gary, unbothered by the mental laser beams she was shooting at his face, soldiered on. "Now hold on just a minute, sweetheart. I really think you should consider letting me sell this house for you. I'll handle everything, you wouldn't have to worry your pretty little head over a single thing. I've got a contract already drawn up for exclusive rights to this house, and won't take but a second of your time to sign it. Mind if I come in? Or better yet, why don't you let me take you out to dinner tonight and we'll celebrate?"

Oh hell no. Is this guy for real?

"Actually, yes, I do mind." Her voice stayed steady despite the hot annoyance pumping through her veins. "I've told you, I'm staying with Kim as my agent. I don't appreciate you coming to my property and not taking *no* for an answer, and I'd like you to leave. Immediately."

"Now, Stefania-" he tried cutting in again, his voice a little louder. She gritted her teeth. *He's really doubling down on the "not taking no for an answer" thing.*

A low, vicious growl emanated from the kitchen, cutting Gary off from whatever nonsense he was about the spew. Stefania leaped on the opportunity.

"My dog doesn't like visitors, Gary, and he's very protective. I won't be able to keep him back if he comes out of the kitchen and decides to attack you. For the last time- do not come on my property or contact me again." She stepped back and quickly slammed the door, relishing the look of fear that flashed across the man's face.

She stayed by the front window and watched the cretin debate whether or not to knock again, then finally turn away and slink into his shiny black Cadillac. *Insufferable man.*

When his taillights disappeared down the driveway, she heaved a sigh and steeled herself for the inevitable conversation with the yeti in her kitchen.

She didn't have much time to prepare. Oswald prowled towards her, crossing the living room in a matter of moments. His glacial eyes glittered with rage and his lips were drawn back in a snarl, baring the full length of his fangs. He looked wild, angry... dangerous.

Stefania took an involuntary step back and pressed herself against the front door. She didn't think he would hurt her, but she hadn't seen him look this furious before. "Oswald?"

His deep growl echoed through her bones as he lifted her off the ground in one swift movement, pulling her into his arms. She yelped with surprise, but he didn't seem to hear it. Instead, he buried his face in her neck and nuzzled her more aggressively than usual. When he spoke, his voice was uneven and full of gravel.

"He wants to take you to dinner? I will tear his limbs off of his body if he touches you."

Stefania blanched at the possessiveness in his tone. She'd known he was growing attached to her, but this jealousy and rage over another man talking to her was not the way to her heart. She ran her hands over his thick furry neck and tried to get him to look at her. "I'm fine, it's fine. He's not a threat."

He snarled again and held her tighter. "You are *mine*."

Okay. That was enough. She gripped his horns and forced his head back so she could look him in the eye. He stilled instantly, the anger in his eyes slowly morphing into lust. "Oswald, you need to calm down. He is *not* a threat. He is an *asshole*, but he is not a threat. I'm not going anywhere with him. Breathe."

He drew in a ragged breath, then another.

"That's good," she coaxed. "Keep breathing for me."

He shifted, his hands creeping down to her hips as he held her gaze. She squeezed his horns in reproach and he spasmed involuntarily, gripping her ass. Her legs wrapped instinctively around his hips and she felt his cock begin to unsheathe against her core.

"Oswald, I appreciate you being protective of me, I really do. But you can't turn into a possessive feral monster every time I speak to a man. It's not healthy. I shouldn't have to put aside my own feelings to manage your emotions and calm you down."

Reminding him of another man had been a mistake, and Oswald's eyes narrowed slightly as he gripped her more firmly, pulling her down on him to grind against her center.

"Stefania, I *am* a monster." The words rumbled out of him in a deep snarl that should *not* have been sexy... but it was. This yeti had been resetting all of her standards for what she considered sexy. "I am *your* monster."

She gasped and closed her eyes, her thin pajamas doing nothing to shield against his long cock rubbing against her, the pleasure building inside her within moments. She rocked against him, seeking friction as the spiral of ecstasy grew and grew.

Suddenly Oswald released her, and she fell back onto the bed. She hadn't even realized that he'd walked them into the bedroom. Before she could even react, he held up a single sharp claw on his left hand and sliced right down the front of her shirt. It flapped open, revealing her breasts. She didn't even have time to gasp before he gave her pants the same treatment, slicing them and her underwear clean off. "Oswald!"

Stefania only had a split second to mourn her favorite pair of pajamas before Oswald lowered his face between her thighs, and all thoughts of clothing fled from her brain. He licked and sucked her through two orgasms, twisting the blunted fingers of his right hand inside her to wring out every bit of pleasure from her body. She could feel him pushing against her as he withdrew his hand, and the thought of him stretching her with his knot instead almost made her come a third time.

Apparently Oswald had the same idea.

He crawled onto the bed and loomed over her, settling his cock at the crook of her thighs. He paused and stared down at her, his expression asking her if he could continue.

She nodded.

He didn't waste any more time. He slid easily inside and he set a brutal pace, pounding into her with a determination she hadn't yet seen from him. If she hadn't been so thoroughly prepped, she'd worry about being sore tomorrow. Each thrust brought his knot against her entrance, and she undulated her hips up to meet his. It felt like he was close to bottoming out inside of her and filling her with the bulge of his knot- just needed to push a little bit more- and she was so caught up in the moment that she mindlessly begged for him to knot her. "Oswald, please fill me. Please give me your knot. Please, *please*... I need it. I need you."

Oswald needed no further encouragement.

His movements stuttered as they always did when he was close, but then he ground down hard against her and slowly circled his hips, and her world shattered a third time just as his knot slipped inside her. She dimly registered his roar as he came, the knot swelling impossibly within her as his cock pulsed with his release.

"*MINE!*"

Oswald rolled them so that she was stretched out on top of him. Both of them lay panting, the haze of lust fading rapidly. Stefania hoisted herself up on an elbow to stare down at where they were joined. The stretch was going to take some getting used to and she was glad he'd prepared her well. *How do women in those monster novels not have fissures in their lady bits? Everything just magically fits. Any bigger than this and my cervix would be crying.* "How long are we going to be stuck together?"

"I do not know. Perhaps fifteen, thirty minutes?"

Stefania flopped back down on his chest, snuggling in for the wait. His purring had settled into a quiet, contented rumble. "This knotting business is mildly inconvenient but definitely enjoyable."

They lay in silence for a bit, Oswald gently carding her hair through his blunted claws while she absentmindedly drew circles in his chest fur.

He finally spoke. "Stefania, I need to ask you something."

She stilled. *Oh no.*

She felt his chest rise on a deep inhale before he asked, "Is it true? Are you selling this house?"

Stefania gulped and her eyes started to burn.

It was time.

She couldn't speak or make eye contact with him. Instead, she closed her eyes, took a long, shuddering breath, and nodded. The rumble in his chest stuttered.

He was quiet for a few moments before he softly spoke again.

"When were you going to tell me?"

The tears began to leak out and drip down her nose. "I'm

sorry," she whispered. "My plan was always to renovate the house and return home to Seattle. I didn't- I couldn't-..." She sniffled and tried again. "I didn't think it mattered at first, and then when we began... experimenting... I didn't know things would progress so fast. I didn't want to ruin the good times we were having with harsh reality. And I thought... I thought you would want a yeti for a partner, not a human. I thought I would be a good time for you, you could learn some things, and then you could go find... someone else."

Oswald sat up suddenly, causing her to straddle him to stay comfortable. She bit back a moan at how the movement made his knot to shift inside her. His tone was incredulous as he told her, "Find someone else? You are my *mate*, Stefania. There will never be another one for me."

His statement shocked her out of her stupor, and she snapped her eyes up to his. "Your *what*?"

"My mate. My heart. From the first moment I scented you, saw you- I knew I needed you. You are mine, and I am yours." He framed his face with his big hands. "Mine. Forever."

Her heart started to pound. "Oswald, we aren't even the same species. I *can't* be your mate." She was beginning to panic. She felt a deep affection for him, had enjoyed her time with him, but the word *mate* now seemed to be so permanent and she couldn't stay... right?

She had known since the start that it was a temporary situation. But he hadn't known that, and she had led him on for weeks. This was her fault. Her selfishness had caused this.

The worst part about this was that she couldn't run away from him- they were still stuck together. His knot showed no sign of softening, and she squirmed uncomfortably atop his thighs. She needed space, needed distance.

He looked at her with pleading eyes. "Would it be so bad to stay here... with me?"

"I... it's not that simple, Oswald. We've been living in a dream. How would it even work? You can't be seen, and I can't be a recluse like Charles was."

"We have been making it work for the past two weeks. Nothing needs to change. You are my mate in all the ways that matter according to yeti-folk. You accepted my courting gifts, we brushed each other, and I knotted you. Our mating is complete."

Her panic reached a whole new level. They were essentially married according to yeti-folk custom? "*What?*"

Before he could reply, she felt his knot contract enough to dislodge them. "Hold that thought, Oswald." She slid off of him and onto the floor, grimacing at the lewd squelch and the soreness she felt. She immediately clamped her thighs together and waddled as fast as she could into the bathroom, trying not to think of the indignity of the entire situation. She knew he would've cleaned her up if she'd asked, but she couldn't. She couldn't ask anything else of him except... except for him to leave.

When she finished, Oswald had righted himself and was waiting for her in the living room. He looked as miserable as she felt. She drew in a deep breath and spoke before he could.

"I think we're both in the wrong here. I didn't tell you I was leaving, and you didn't tell me that we are basically *married* according to your customs. I didn't consent to that, Oswald!" Her voice broke on a sob, and she heaved in a shuddering breath.

He reared back like he had been struck, devastation written in his features. "Stefania... I did not... please, *mērō muṭu,* let me explain." He reached for her, but she took a step back.

"No, Oswald... I need space. I need to process everything. You should've told me what all those little presents were and what knotting meant to you. I'm sorry that I hurt you and that I let it get this far without telling you I'm selling the house. I never meant for any of this to happen. But I need for you to go home."

His features crumpled a bit more, and his purring stuttered again. "Stefania... *you* are my home."

She felt her heart crack from that statement as she fought back more tears. "I'm sorry, Oswald. I can't be that for you right now. You should go. Please, give me space."

He flinched, and she had to stop herself from reaching out to him. The room fell silent, his chest no longer making its contented purr, and she mourned its loss. He stared at her for a few more moments, then nodded slowly and turned to the front door.

And then he was gone.

Stefania lowered the blinds in the bathroom window and showered, her movements mechanical as she numbly washed away the evidence of their joining. As she dried herself off, one thought kept recurring in her brain, over and over.

I need to leave. I need to leave. I need to leave.

Before she could talk herself into staying, she haphazardly threw her laptop and clothes into her suitcase, turned out all the lights, and walked out to the garage to throw the luggage in the old truck. When she pulled out of the garage, she turned and looked at the cabin for one last time. She'd miss it fiercely- all the love and work she had thrown into it had made it her personal refuge, but it had always been the plan to leave, so she was leaving. That was what she wanted... right?

She peered into the trees. If Oswald was close by, he wasn't stopping her.

So Stefania left the cabin and the yeti behind.

She drove her truck to the lawyer's office in a daze. All of the Platts and their employees were apparently out to lunch, so she left a hastily scrawled note and the keys to the truck in an envelope and shoved it through the mail flap.

She gazed down the street at Beans, Beans and the Winterhaven Market- she couldn't face Ana and Bridget in her current state. Instead, she turned in the direction of the train station and began to walk, dragging her suitcase behind her.

She just had to make it to Seattle. Once she was safe in her apartment, she could allow herself to fall apart.

Chapter 17

Oswald

Oswald sat in the snow in the forest, peering at the empty cabin through the trees from his favorite hiding spot. It was the same spot where he'd watched Stefania those first weeks. Had it only been a month since he'd rescued her from that bear?

He noted the fresh tire tracks leaving out of the garage and frowned. The sun was setting, and he knew she didn't really like driving when it was this dark and cold. She would be home soon, and he hoped she was done with needing her space. What about his needs, after all? He needed her like he needed to breathe- she was ensconced in his very soul, and every second away from her felt like an eternity.

Hours passed and the house remained dark. No lights shone from the colorful strings on the front porch or from their carefully decorated Christmas tree. The cabin was devoid of life.

Oswald resisted barging into the house and waiting for her in there. She wanted *space*, and he would not go into her home unless invited.

The night wore on, and Stefania did not come home.

Sick with worry, Oswald dashed alongside the roads and into Winterhaven, not bothering to cover his tracks. At the speed he was going, they probably resembled bear prints if no one looked too closely. He covered the distance in record time and stumbled around the outskirts of the town, going from hiding spot to hiding spot with no luck. The truck was nowhere to be seen, and he couldn't catch any trace of her scent.

Where was Stefania?

When he was sure no one was looking, he skirted along the side of Beans, Beans to peer into the front window. He knew she liked the little blonde woman that worked here, perhaps she would've come here for food.

But there was nothing. The bakery was closed, the lights off and chairs resting on the tables. Perhaps she had gone to her friend Ana's house, but Oswald didn't know where that was.

He should've followed her the second she'd left the house upset.

His paws shook as his adrenaline crashed and worst-case scenarios began to play in his head. Was she okay? What if she had been in an accident on the snowy roads? The temperature was well below freezing and her human body was so fragile. Was she cold? Hungry? Stranded? Injured?

He forced himself to take several deep breaths. At this rate, he could spend all night frantically searching the miles and miles of roadsides for her if he kept up this train of thought. *No*, he concluded, it was best if he kept himself calm and returned to the house. She was getting the space she requested, and he needed to trust that she was safe instead of continuing to spiral.

His shoulders slumped in defeat, Oswald trudged back to the cabin and sat in his hiding place, waiting.

And waiting.

She never came home.

For four days he held vigil outside of her cabin, refusing to leave that spot just in case she came back. He had no appetite and only his body's instinct for survival had him scooping up snow for hydration. He slept very little, only falling asleep when exhaustion took over, then jolting awake at the slightest noise. Once, a car came down the driveway and he almost ran out to meet it, only to catch himself at the last moment when it was just her two friends. He'd scuttled back into the forest and they had disappeared into the house, emerging an hour later with multiple boxes of what smelled like food.

He settled back into his spot and continued to wait. He wanted to be the first thing Stefania saw when she returned. He'd apologize to her on his knees and beg her to forgive him. He would explain everything- the carvings, the brushing, the knotting. She deserved to know it all and to make her own choice.

He now realized how much he had deceived her in the plot to claim her as his own mate. Yes, she had not been truthful about selling the house- and the land his home was on- but he had never asked about her plans for the future. He had assumed that she was moving there permanently, and that they could live happily ever after. In all their easy conversations, the subject of the future had rarely been breached. They talked about their upbringings, their interests- but no plans for the future had ever been discussed besides vague statements. He realized now that she had avoided the topic, and he had gone along with it willingly.

And what if she chose to end it? What if she didn't love him or want him for a mate? Oswald knew that he was most likely more attached to her than she was to him. There was a chance that she just viewed him as a novelty, or like one of the fictional characters in the smutty books she read. But he was very real, and very much in love with her. His body had recognized her as his mate from the instant she had stepped foot onto the property, and that had sealed his fate. She was it for him- there would never be another. But he would give her the power to reject the mating, even if it broke his heart to do so.

But on the morning of the fifth day, a terrible realization

struck him.

She wasn't coming back.

She'd already rejected him.

She had left.

She had left him, left the cabin, left Alaska.

All without saying goodbye.

A deep ache settling in his silent chest, Oswald slowly dragged himself from the ground and went in search of the spare key, hidden under a rock near the garage. He didn't like the idea of going in the house without her, but the desire to know if she truly was gone outweighed any sense of reluctance. Sure enough, the house was empty of most of her belongings, her clothing and luggage all missing. Even the refrigerator and pantry had been cleaned out, and it didn't take him long to realize the reason for her friends' visit a few days ago.

It was all the confirmation he needed.

She was not planning on returning.

He wandered aimlessly through the house, staring blankly at his surroundings. Almost all of the carvings remained, including *The Hug*. His chest felt as if it was caving in- she'd fully rejected him according to yeti-folk traditions, whether she realized it or not. Only one item was missing from the house- the wooden bracelet he had so painstakingly inscribed with tiny letters.

He gathered the rest of the courting gifts into a grocery bag, intending to take them to his small home and turn them into scrap or burn them if she never came back. Instead, he found himself placing them all on a shelf next to his bed so he could stare at them before attempting to sleep.

Sleep did not come easily.

Time passed, the days bleeding into each other. He rarely left his cabin to hunt, deciding instead to use his stash of preserved meats to feed himself, although his appetite remained nonexistent. He had no desire to carve, spending the days moping around his small space and staring at the shelf of figurines. He forced himself to shower to keep his fur clean, but each time he was pelted with memories of Stefania in his bathroom the night he rescued her.

Everything reminded him of Stefania. His shower, his hairbrush, even his bed where he'd kept her warm that fateful night. He told himself that this would pass- but it felt like he was just lying to himself.

His chest remained silent, a physical reminder of his depression. He'd gotten used to the constant rumbling (his "purr", as Stefania had called it), and he felt incomplete without it.

He felt incomplete without *her*.

His mate was gone, his heart torn asunder. No, not *his mate*- she had rejected the mating. He had to stop thinking of her as such.

He had never known so much joy as he had in the past month, only now to be faced with the greatest sorrow he had ever felt besides the death of his parents. But this situation with Stefania- unlike their deaths- this was *his* fault, and he knew it. If only he hadn't come on so strong. If only he'd been more patient.

If only he were human, not a monster.

As he languished in his cabin, a small part of Oswald knew he needed to make a plan for the future. If she was really gone, he understood that it was only a matter of time before someone bought the property and he would be forced to leave. He would lose his home and his workshop- he couldn't risk staying and being seen by any other humans. He'd taken a huge risk with Stefania that had paid off, but he doubted the new owner would be amenable to having a woodworking yeti living next door.

Where would he go?

Alaska was his home, but after being with Stefania for those few happy weeks, he realized his previous existence here had been so lonely. Could he make the trek back to the Himalayas by himself? Would he even know how to fit in with the other yeti-folk? He knew the basic customs in theory, but putting them to practice might be difficult. What if he went all that way only to be rejected by the clans?

He didn't think they would do such a thing, but there was no way to know for sure, and the thought of being rejected again was agonizing.

Could he go to Seattle and try to find Stefania? He recognized that idea as highly impractical the second it crossed his mind- it was impossible for him to hide in such a big city. And it felt a little stalker-ish to travel that far when she had made it clear that she didn't want him, although he could admit to himself now that he had fully been in stalker mode during the first few weeks after her arrival in Winterhaven. He blamed it on the uncontrollable yeti hormones, driven mindless by the bestial need to stake a claim on her. But he'd fought against that and gained a semblance of control the more he was around her, wanting to be the partner she deserved, hoping she would see past his fur and fangs to the soul beneath the surface. And the more he got to talk to her, to truly *know* her, the more he fell in love with all that she was.

She was everything to him. Yes, she was beautiful and her scent mouth-watering, but she was so much more than that. She was kind, generous, loving, artistic, and open-hearted- their shared intimacy in even the smallest of moments had been more than he could have ever hoped for. With everything they had done together, he had thought for sure that she loved him.

And yet, it had all fallen to pieces in a matter of moments.

And she had left.

Chapter 18

Stefania

It didn't take Stefania long to realize that she had royally screwed up.

She sat on her couch after work, staring at the white walls of her apartment. She had been home for a week, and she had done everything she could to try and resume her old life. She went into the office every day and saw coworkers who hadn't even noticed that she had been gone for over six weeks, not to mention the security guard who had tried to make her sign in as a visitor the first few days she was back. Was she that invisible, or had she held everyone at arm's length?

No one in Seattle had missed her.

Ana and Bridget had not given up on her- no, they texted her every day without fail. The three of them had a group chat titled *The Wintermavens*, and getting messages from them was the highlight of her days. They didn't try to guilt her into coming back or press her for more information on why she had left so suddenly- instead, they quietly supported her and told her they would be there for her when- and if- she was ready to share. She wanted desperately to tell them everything about Oswald, to share her pain and heartbreak and tell them to look after him.

Oswald...

She fiddled with the wooden bracelet that encircled her wrist, and her fingertips brushed over the engraving. She hadn't taken it off except to shower and sleep. Regret swirled through her at leaving the rest of her carvings in the cabin, especially now that she knew what they symbolized- what would Oswald think if he knew she left them there? Had he gone into the house and found them all?

She knew she should not have left Alaska so suddenly, but everything had come crashing down on her at once. His declaration that they were mates had shaken her to her very core- how was she supposed to process that information? Running away had not been the best answer, but time and distance had brought some much-needed clarity to the situation.

I've been sleeping with a yeti.

A yeti that thinks I'm his mate.

And I miss him terribly.

Did he only like her because he was codependent on her? It wasn't the first time she had wondered if he had just latched on to the first semblance of kindness he was shown. His mate probably could've been any other woman- Stefania just happened to be a conveniently single female that had taken over Charles' property.

She frowned and shook her head. No, that didn't seem to be true. The connection they had was deeper than surface level attraction. They had bonded over shared interests like art and food, and had lively conversations on a wide variety of topics. He'd been the artist that carved *The Hug*- the statue that conveyed such a sense of affection and belonging between two souls. She was doing him a disservice to even think about him as a mindless feral creature that only cared about rutting random women. He was an intelligent, sensitive being.

He cared about her- she wasn't just a convenient female to him. She knew that, deep in her soul.

Besides, he probably had been in close proximity to other humans before- close enough to smell them and stalk them. But he had chosen to follow *her*, save *her*, to reveal himself to *her*- no other. It had been *her* scent that had driven him wild with lust.

Stefania closed her eyes as she remembered the mind-blowing sex. How on earth could she ever fathom being with another man? There was no doubt in her mind- Oswald had been a superior lover in every way compared to any of the men in her past. She loved that she had the ability to turn him on in an instant- it was such an ego boost that he found her irresistible.

He was gentle, kind, and thoughtful. He was her protector, lover, and friend.

She hugged a throw pillow to her chest as the realization crashed over her.

Oh, crap... I love him.

She loved her yeti. He was everything she could've ever wanted in a partner- he just happened to be a different species. She loved his fangs, his claws, his fur, and even the sheer size of him that made her- a tall, curvaceous woman- feel downright petite. She loved the way he volunteered to do dishes after she cooked, the way he chopped wood for her after a blizzard, the way he held her in his powerful arms at night as if she was the most precious thing in the world to him. But more importantly, she loved the mind behind those beautiful blue eyes.

So why wasn't she in Winterhaven with him, where she belonged?

As she gazed around at her apartment, it became clear to her. This apartment, this city… it wasn't where she wanted to be any more. It was no longer home.

She picked up her phone and called Kim.

She arrived in Winterhaven with as little fuss as she did the first time- but this time, Ana and Bridget were both waiting for her at the train station, both bundled up against an impending snow storm. The emotions from the past few weeks caught up to her as she hugged them both fiercely, and she tried to disguise her tears as happy ones.

Ana and Bridget exchanged a glance that told her she wasn't fooling them, but they didn't press for details. Instead, they gently pushed her into Ana's car and said that when she was ready to talk, they would listen. She filled them in on the past two dreadful weeks, finally telling them that she planned to stay in Winterhaven, and happy tears did leak out of all three of them.

When they arrived at the cabin, Ana gave Stefania a few grocery bags of essentials. "The storm shouldn't be too bad tonight, but most everything will be closed for Christmas tomorrow. This will get you through the next few days. I've restocked you with that good coffee you like, too." She winked at Stefania.

Bridget pumped her arms in the air like a cheerleader. "The Wintermavens are reunited! We're so glad you're back and here to stay!"

Stefania embraced them both, choking back more tears. "I'm so happy to be home. Merry Christmas, you two. Be careful and text me when you both are home!"

She dashed up the icy stairs of the porch as carefully as she could while carrying the grocery bags and her suitcase. The wind was bitterly cold and howled through the trees as she unlocked the door, then turned and waved goodbye to Ana and Bridget.

The house was dark, cold, and empty. She had half expected Oswald to be there waiting for her, but of course he wasn't- why would he stay when she was gone? Her heart skipped a beat. *What if he left Winterhaven entirely? Would he do that?*

The familiar ache bloomed in her chest. Was she alone again?

157

Logically she knew that just as Oswald hadn't chosen her because of convenience, she hadn't latched onto him simply so she wouldn't be alone. She had molded herself into someone like her mother who didn't need a *man* to feel complete, but she felt a connection with the yeti unlike anything she had felt before. In her rush to get back to Winterhaven, she hadn't even considered the fact that he might not even be here.

If he was gone, truly gone- she'd never find him.

She knew it was too risky to go out and look for him now, so she turned on all the Christmas decorations and hoped that if he was around, he would see it and come back to her. She hoped she wasn't too late.

And so, she put away the groceries and waited.

Stefania sat on the couch hours later, trying and failing to not wallow in despair. Earlier, she noticed that all her carvings- the *courting gifts,* as Oswald had called them- were gone. *The Hug* was missing from the dining room table, and the little lily box had disappeared from her dresser along with the comb and with the rest of the presents he had left her. He must've taken them- did this mean he rescinded his courtship? She didn't know enough about the yeti-folk courting habits.

Has he given up on me?

She couldn't blame him if he had. She had left him without a single word, taking the cowardly way out. Was she even worth waiting for?

Some Christmas Eve this was. Even her favorite holiday movie, *White Christmas,* was failing to cheer her up. Danny Kaye was just beginning to sing about choreography when she heard it- a noise outside on the porch.

Stefania sat up and hurried to the door. The snowstorm was in full force and almost no one in their right mind would venture out in such weather. But standing on her front porch was none other than the yeti that she had just spent hours worrying about.

She opened the door and they stared at each other without a word. The intense numbing cold immediately swirled inside, and she didn't even notice.

He was here. He was safe.

Would he forgive her?

They both heard his chest begin to rumble at the same time, breaking the spell. She couldn't help it- she flung herself into his arms, and he caught her midair and hauled her against him. He was covered in snow and ice and she didn't care one bit.

He was *here*.

She squeezed her eyes shut and buried her face in his neck, trying to control the sobs that were threatening to break free. He crushed her to his chest and the purring vibrations soothed something in her soul. She was where she belonged, and all was right in the world.

She barely registered the change in temperature as he moved them inside and shut the door with a kick.

"I am so *sorry*, Oswald." Her voice broke, but she gamely kept going. "I didn't mean to hurt you. I was upset and scared, which is not an excuse to cause you pain. I should have stayed and talked it over with you, but I panicked. I'm so sorry."

She could feel him shake his head, and his deep voice reverberated through her. "It is I who hurt you, Stefania. I did not disclose the true meaning behind my gifts. It was wrong of me to keep such knowledge from you." Anguish laced every one of his words. "I coveted you and courted you without your consent. For that, I am deeply, deeply sorry."

He set her down in front of the fireplace and knelt before her, running his palms up her legs. "Please forgive me, *mērō muṭu*."

She wiped her cheeks with the backs of her hands, took a deep breath, and just *looked* at him. At first glance, he seemed the same as he always appeared to her. Strong, solid, and steady- and yet his expression seemed haunted, his beautiful glacial eyes sad. *She* had put that sadness there. "Can we forgive each other? I promise not to run away the next time I get scared. If we're going to do this, permanently..." She paused at the look of hope that flashed across his face, and she tried for a watery smile. "We'll need to talk some things out. The jealousy, possessiveness- we'll have to work on that. You'll have to trust that I..." she trailed off. Could she say it?

He took her hands in his and waited patiently for her to continue.

Just tell him.

"I... I love you, Oswald."

His eyes went wide with shock, and he seemed to stop breathing. She barreled on. "I don't know what the future holds, but I know that I love you and I don't want to live without you. Going back to Seattle and seeing how lonely I was made me realize what I've found here in Winterhaven- a family. I've found friends who love me without judgment and a partner who welded together the broken pieces of my heart. I've made this place into my home, and I don't want to be anywhere else." She shivered. "Even if I do wish it was warmer here."

Oswald's eyes flicked to her chest, lingering. Her cold, wet pajamas were plastered to her and were beginning to catch his attention. His gaze returned to her face and she could see the lust clouding his expression. But he spoke gently, caressing the backs of her hands with his thumbs. "I love you, my sweet Stefania. I want nothing more than to be with you for the rest of our lives. And I cannot promise that I will not make more mistakes- I am, at my core, a beast- but I promise to try and control my instincts. This is as new to me as it is to you, and I will do my best to be the yeti you deserve."

She wrapped her arms around his neck. "We'll figure this out together, okay?"

Oswald hugged her around her waist, his head settling against her chest. After a few moments he nuzzled between her breasts, breaking any remaining tension and causing her to laugh. He spoke, his voice coming out muffled from where he was pressed against her. "I am sorry, I just cannot help myself. I have missed you." He looked up and her and grinned, baring those cute fangs that she adored so much. "And your breasts."

She stroked the base of one of his horns and he shuddered. "I've missed you too. Should I show you how much?"

He stood and effortlessly flung her over a shoulder in one smooth motion, striding off to the bedroom. "First, I will show you. Many, many times."

Christmas morning dawned bright and beautiful. The storm had cleared out, leaving the landscape blanketed in a few inches of fresh snow that glittered in the sunlight.

They stayed in bed a while, cuddling and slowly teasing each other until Oswald had growled and hoisted her up his body until she sat perched on his face. She'd taken his knot last night and was a little too sore to take it again, but after she rode his face, she slid down and returned the favor. After he came apart with a window-rattling roar, they showered and Stefania cooked a big Christmas breakfast of bacon, eggs, and pancakes.

She made sure to send a text to the *Wintermavens* group chat to thank them again for their thoughtfulness, and they made plans to meet up the day after tomorrow for another movie night.

When breakfast was eaten and the dishes were put away, Oswald sat on the couch and drew her to him. "I have something for you." His deep voice caused her to shiver in anticipation, and he presented her with a small package. It was covered in the same paper that the rest of his gifts had been wrapped in, and she reached for it with a shaky hand.

"I didn't mean to leave your carvings here. I wasn't really thinking straight when I left." She opened the paper and gasped. Inside was a miniature version of *The Hug*, except this time, there was a very clear difference in the figures. One figure was a woman, and the other was very much shaped like a yeti. If you only glanced at it, it could be mistaken for a man- but Stefania knew.

It was the two of them, entwined forever in a loving embrace.

She brought the figurine closer to her face to inspect it. It was beautiful, something only the hands and soul of an artist would be able to make. She stroked a hand across the smooth wood. "Oswald, this is... this is stunning. It's so beautiful."

"I know how much you love the original, but I wanted to make you a special one as a mating present." He ducked his head. "I was supposed to give it to you the day after I... well, after you took my knot."

She hugged the carving to her chest, then reached down to put it on the coffee table. "I brought you something for Christmas. It's just a little something, but I hope you'll enjoy it. It doesn't even compare to this beautiful statue." She'd found him a book on different wood carving techniques in the Anchorage airport- she wasn't even sure if he already knew them, but she thought the book was neat and hoped he liked it.

Oswald nuzzled her affectionately. "I am sure I will like whatever you give me. I will open it later, but right now I do not want to let you go. I am very glad you came home, my sweet Stefania."

She smiled. "I am too. I'll still have to go back to Seattle at some point and pack up all of my things. Bridget and Ana said they would fly with me to Seattle and we'll road trip back up through Canada with my car and a moving van. Although honestly, I think it will be mostly clothing so I might not even need the van. I'll probably sell or donate all of my furniture." She patted the leather couch. "I'm rather attached to all of the furniture here."

"How long do you think you would be gone?"

She shrugged and sifted through some of the fur on his chest. His rolling purr was a balm to her soul- she hadn't realized how much she'd missed it. "A week, maybe a little more. It's a long drive up through the Canadian Rockies and I'd like to sightsee a little bit. The area around Banff is supposed to be beautiful." Stefania paused, looking back up at him. "Will you be okay for that long?"

He smiled. "I will be better this time, knowing you are coming back to me. And I am glad you are taking your two friends with you, it will be safer."

"Oswald... do you think at some point in time, you might be comfortable with me telling them about you?"

She felt him tense under her. "You want to tell your friends... about *me*?"

"I don't want to keep any secrets from them. I trust them, and I don't think they would tell anyone." She laughed. "We've all read enough alien smut, I think they would be more surprised to find out ycti-folk are real than to judge me for falling in love with one."

His breath hitched and he ran his claws gently through her hair. "I do not think I will ever tire of hearing you say that you love me."

Stefania grinned up at him. "I love you, Oswald. You are amazingly kind and sweet and I want to be able to show you off to my friends. We'll be careful about it- I'll make sure you're protected."

He growled and palmed her ass playfully. "That is *my* job- to protect you."

"Good partners protect *each other*." She swatted his hand away and tweaked one of his fangs. He nipped at her in response and she giggled. "You can protect me from bears and snowstorms, and I'll protect you from the outside world. But I want to be able to invite a few friends over without you having to hide. They'll love you like I do."

She could tell he was considering it, but didn't want to push him any further today. She understood that it was a huge risk and so many things could go wrong, but she didn't think Ana or Bridget would ever betray her trust. But if she was to stay in

Winterhaven, she couldn't fathom lying to her closest friends for the rest of her life. "Just think about it. You don't have to give me an answer right away. I'm just excited for our future together."

Oswald gazed at her, his heart shining in his bright blue eyes.

"I never could have imagined having a mate such as you, *mērō muṭu*. You have given me such joy and hope, and whatever I can do to make sure you are as happy as I am, I will do. If you want to tell your friends, we can tell your friends."

He leaned forward, touching his forehead to hers. "You are mine, and I am yours. Forever."

Tears of joy pricked at her eyes as she repeated the words back to him. "You are mine, and I am yours. Forever."

She wrapped her arms around his neck and they held each other tightly.

"Merry Christmas, Oswald."

"Merry Christmas, Stefania."

It was the best Christmas she'd had in a very long time.

Epilogue

Stefania lounged in a chair in Beans, Beans, nursing a cappuccino and a chocolate croissant. Bridget had just closed the coffee shop early and was sweeping the floor.

"Really, Bridget, I can help if you just tell me what to do."

Bridget waved her away and continued to sweep. "You're doing me a favor just by keeping me company. It can be awfully tedious to close this place up by myself."

Stefania took a sip of her cappuccino. "Don't you have an employee who can close with you? Or even close *for* you?"

"I do, but they normally work the early morning shifts when the crowds rush in. And I really don't mind, most of the time I just put on music and dance around as I clean. Makes it go by a little bit faster."

Stefania smiled at that. She could easily picture the curvy little blonde dancing around the tables, using the broomstick as a mock partner. "I'm sure the people walking by enjoy that view."

Bridget laughed and patted the bandana she was using as a headband. "I doubt anyone really wants to see me dancing around this sweaty and gross."

A knock sounded and both of their gazes swung towards the locked door.

The eldest Platt brother stood outside, holding up a big brown envelope. Stefania heard Bridget's small intake of breath. "What's he doing here?"

Stefania set down her cup. "He might be here for me- I've been meaning to stop by the office and pick up the keys to the truck but I keep forgetting. It's just been so much easier to use the snowmobile this week."

Bridget walked to the door, patting her headband and fussing with her hot pink apron. She unlocked it and held the door open for the Platt brother.

He inhaled and stared down at Bridget for a moment, who seemed to be speechless in his presence. She couldn't blame Bridget- the man was objectively handsome. Tall, bearded, and broad-shouldered, he was built like he was more suited for a football field or a lumberjack competition than for a courtroom.

Then his gaze snapped to Stefania and he stepped inside the shop. Bridget seemed to come back to her senses and drew in a deep breath, her voice slightly higher pitched as she asked, "Would you like any coffee? I've just cleaned the machine but I'd be happy to make you something."

"No, thank you. I just need to drop this off with Ms. Clarke." He stalked forward and handed the envelope to Stefania. "I saw your snowmobile was still outside and wanted to give this to you. Your uncle left a special letter with us. It was to be given to you only in the event that you decided to keep the property and stay in Winterhaven."

She gaped at him. Charles had left her another letter, and she never would have gotten to read it if she'd sold the house? "Did he leave any more surprises with you, or is this the last of it?"

The lawyer smirked slightly. "This is the only other thing he left with us. The keys to the truck are also in the envelope. His file is now considered closed."

She sat back in her chair and stared at the envelope, turning it over in her hands. The eldest Platt turned and headed towards the door, nodding to Bridget on his way out. "Happy New Year!" the little blonde called to him.

He paused in the doorway but did not look back. "Same to you, Ms. Byrne."

Stefania and Bridget both watched him walk back towards the law office. Stefania turned and grinned at her friend. "Ohhh, you *like* him!"

Bridget rolled her eyes and glared at Stefania. "Shut up. Who wouldn't like any of the Platt brothers? They're all hot."

"Are any of them married?"

"As far as I know, no. I don't think any of them have dated around here, though. They must go to Fairbanks or Anchorage to date."

Stefania quietly mulled that over as she studied the envelope in her hands. Bridget resumed sweeping, glancing over at Stefania. "Are you going to open that now?"

Stefania shoved her chocolate croissant in the little paper bag and stood, grabbing her thick parka off the back of the chair. "I think I'll open it at home, if that's okay. I'm going to drive the snowmobile home- do you mind coming to get me sometime this week so I can grab the truck out of the Platt's parking garage?"

Bridget nodded. "That's fine, just let me know when. I don't have any big catering gigs this week now that the holidays are over, so I'm free in the afternoons."

Stefania pulled on all of her heavy winter clothes and trudged to the door. "Thanks for the coffee and croissant. I'll text you about the truck. Try not to swoon over any more Platt brothers."

She grinned at the mock outrage on her friend's face as she left the coffee shop.

Dear Stefania,

If you are receiving this letter, then you must have decided to keep the cabin and remain in Winterhaven. I hope you love this little town as much as I did. You may wonder why I left the property to you, even if we never met, but you are my last surviving relative and so it should go to you.

I was born to strict parents, both fresh off the boat from Ireland. We lived in New York City for my entire childhood, alongside many other immigrant families. Among our neighbors lived a girl a year younger than I, a beautiful dark-haired lass named Isabelle. Our families were rivals, but to this day I do not know why they disliked each other. It could've been something as simple as a misunderstanding that got out of hand. I will never know.

Isabelle and I kept our friendship a secret for many years, communicating through passed notes and stolen moments. As we got older, we fell in love. One thing led to another, as it tends to do, and we became secretly engaged.

We were both so young- she was nineteen to my twenty. We thought we knew everything, and all that mattered was our love. We wanted out of the city- to live somewhere we could see the sky, with clean rivers and forests, and maybe even mountains covered in snow. I worked extra hours on the docks to save money for us to escape together.

We were on our way out of the city, heading to our new life, when the accident happened. Even years later, it is too painful to describe what happened or the aftermath, so I will simply say that I lost my entire heart that day.

When our families discovered what had taken place, the neighborhood went into an uproar. Her family wanted to kill me- and instead of protecting me, my family threw me into the street and ceased all contact with me. To them, I had betrayed them- they were not willing to listen to me talk about the love of my life. My little brother was just a small child at that time- I don't know what they told him about me, if they told him anything at all. It's possible they may have told him that I was never his brother and forbid him to speak of me. My parents- your great-grandparents- were not evil people, but times were different and loyalty to the family was considered top priority.

Between the very real threat to my life and the memories of Isabelle, I could not remain in New York City any longer. Instead, I exiled myself to the farthest corner of the continent and threw myself into a career in deep-sea fishing off the coast of Alaska. It is a dangerous business, and I did not really care if I lived or died. I had nothing more to lose.

Much to my dismay, I survived.

When I got too old and arthritic for my body to deal with the rigors of ship life, I came here to Winterhaven, to be at the base of Denali. Isabelle would've loved it here. I've kept mainly to myself throughout the years, leading a quiet existence as my penance for my misspent youth.

In retrospect, I have done a disservice to Isabelle's memory in never speaking of her. But I have lived with the pain and guilt of that accident for many years, and when you live with something like that for so long, it is difficult to break the cycle and move past it. And so, I never really did. I harbored a deep resentment towards my parents for disowning me and thought they all hated me. But when I received my diagnosis and began to stare down the barrel of my own mortality, I decided to track down the family, only to learn that almost everyone was gone- except for you.

Were you to simply sell the property and return to your life in Seattle, then I was content to let the memory of me, one sad old man, float away into oblivion. But as luck would have it, you have decided to stay in Winterhaven. This town is truly that- a haven for all those who need one.

I hope you find what you need here, Stefania. I hope that you'll take the cabin and personalize it however you like it- it's your home now. And if Henry hasn't introduced yourself already, he will soon. He's been itching to make improvements on that cabin, but as I am an old man with no sense of style (as Ben would often tell me), it suited my needs just fine. And if Henry tells you that he always won our backgammon matches, don't believe him.

You may or may not have met Oswald by now. Oswald is unlike anyone you have most likely met before, and he is a dear, dear friend. If you have not, I hope that when you do, you are able to look past appearances and into the soul beneath. He has been by my side for many years now. He has the biggest heart in the world, perhaps literally, and I think he could use a friend like you.

He may say that I saved him, but he saved me, too.

And now, I shall draw this rather dramatic letter to a close. If you take anything away from this letter, Stefania, it is to not do as I did. Do not let sadness and bitterness drive you away from those that matter the most to you.

Love whoever you want as much as you can, for as long as you can.

Do not feel sad for me, Stefania. I go to my Isabelle, and I am ready.

Charles

Stefania sat with Oswald on the couch, the letter in her hands. Both of them were quiet for long moments. "Did Charles ever mention anything about this to you?"

Oswald shook his head. "No, nothing. I did not realize he was so secretive, but he never mentioned anything about his past to me. I never thought to pry, but sometimes I wonder if I ever knew him."

She heard the sadness and hurt in his deep voice. Charles had been his friend, his family- to be friends with someone for that long but feel like your relationship had been only surface level? This was why she did not want to keep Oswald a secret from Ana and Bridget for too long.

She climbed into his lap and wrapped her arms around his neck. Hugs weren't the answer to everything, but they certainly didn't hurt.

"I won't keep any secrets from you." Her whisper was

barely audible, but his arms tightened around her in response. "You already know me better than anyone in the world, and I love you. Whatever happens in the future, we'll both know about it, and we'll face it together."

"Together," he echoed.

Acknowledgements

I want to thank all of my friends individually, but it will take many, many pages to express my love and devotion to all of you. Just know that if you are in my life, I am eternally grateful for you. Yes, YOU. Thank you. (If you think this is about you, it is.) Also, I can't believe you read this book. I'm sorry???? We never have to talk about it if you don't want to.

To my partner: You are the most patient, supportive man in the world. I appreciate everything you've ever done for me and for indulging me in all the smutty audiobooks we listen to. I can't wait until you listen to this one and laugh with me at the things that came out of my brain.

To Megan: Thank you for beta reading, for cheering me on when I got into my head, for letting me work out my thoughts in endless texts, and for the absolutely stunning cover art. I love it and want to stare at it for all eternity. I could not have done this without you.

To Brittany: Thank you for all our themed movie nights and our never-ending shared love of Mr. Darcy. You are the wind beneath my wings.

To Heather: Thank you for your love and endless support. I feel like you are my personal cheering section and I feel the love from afar. We're going to invent a transporter soon.

To Elizabeth: Your pep talks never fail to cheer me up. I love you and thank you for letting me lean so heavily on you when the imposter syndrome is kicking in.

To the group chat (LH, DB, DA, BB, MB): This is for y'all. Love you all and I'm so appreciative of your support. This definitely would not have been written without you!

To my mother: Thank you for being the most supportive mother a child could ever have. I love you. Please don't read this book.

Author: Jade Dara

Jade wrote her first novel at the tender age of twelve. While that book has never been published and life got in the way of writing, she always yearned for ~~the mines~~ *cough* the opportunity to create new worlds and new characters. She resides in the Carolinas with her very supportive manflesh and her very needy pit bull, and dreams of one day writing full-time in a hammock by a lake.

Instagram: @jade.dara.author
Email: jade.dara.author@gmail.com

If you'd like to share the love, please leave a review!